AIR FOR FIRE

AIR
FOR
FIRE

MAJOR

A DISTANT MIRROR

AIR FOR FIRE
© the author, 2017

ISBN 978-0-9807706-6-7

Web adistantmirror.com.au
Email admin@adistantmirror.com.au

By the same author
THE DAY OF THE NEFILIM

STORIES

POEMS

STORIES

HYPATIA (b. 350–370 – d. March 415 A.D.) was a
Neoplatonist philosopher and scientist, and a
leading academic and teacher in Alexandria, in the
Roman province of Egypt. Her students came from
all over the known world, from both inside and
outside the Roman Empire. She admitted both
Christians and pagans to her classes — she
apparently observed no distinction between the
two — as well as both men and women.

Alexandria was one of the main centres of early
Christianity, while still having a large and active
pagan community. Hypatia became involved in a
political dispute between Cyril, the Christian
Patriach of the city, and Orestes, the Roman
Prefect, who was a pagan.

Her death was ordered by Cyril (who is
now Saint Cyril, a Catholic 'Church Father'),
in 415 A.D.

A Christian mob attacked her outside her house,
and dragged her to a church. There, they flayed her
with seashells and pottery shards, then dragged her
through the streets, before dismembering and
burning her. At which stage of this torture she died
will never be known, but one account describes her
'convulsing limbs being torn from her flayed body'.

AIR FOR FIRE

THOSE WHO HAD SURVIVED the flood by taking to the mountains or the tops of the highest hills returned to the valleys and plains, and there they found that everything was covered with silt and mud and debris, and they sighed and set to work.

And even though the heat of the sun would sometimes dry the land until it cracked, and other times the rain would come so heavily that the crops were washed away, life went on. Somewhere, animals and seed had survived and what was needed for building was found, and so, although life was harder than it had been before the change, and it was uncertain, it did go on.

But that was all a very long time ago. Things settled down. Today, we have order.

*

"Cardinal Synesius," — I have been asked more than once, in so many words — "you were close to the pagan Hypatia, one of her students — what really happened? And how is it that you have become a Cardinal?"

Very well, I shall break my silence. Here is what happened concerning the pagan Hypatia.

*

"Librarian..."

I am watching the approaching Walkers from the main window of the Soil Feeder Archive. They clank, wheezing steam and smoke, through the corn fields; the foliage thrust aside by their iron flanks, rows crushed beneath their riveted hooves, their crews unaware or uncaring of the damage they are doing to the crops.

I hear her sigh. She has come to stand beside me. "What do they want now? Are we expecting anything?" She says it to herself; there is no use asking me.

Librarian Hypatia is... well, one of *them*. Half born, half made. She is a relic of the old world; we don't grow them like her any more, and we certainly don't *make* them like her any more — not that we could; even if we wanted to. We don't stand as straight or tall, we don't think as fast, and we don't remake ourselves the way they are built to. They are from the past, a past not like anything you or I have ever known. Most people these days don't talk about the ones like her. Me? Oh, *I* want to know...

Hypatia has been the Head Librarian at the Serapeum since her predecessor became something to do with the Cardinals (apparently an offer he could not refuse). He taught her well; she knows where every Soil Conditioner, every Enhancer, every Charm and Relic, every Amulet, every Air, Karma and Water Filter and every book and scroll is kept. I think that the entire contents of the Serapeum Library are catalogued in her mind. And I get the feeling that she understands it all, as well.

When the Walkers bring in shipments from the Cardinals' factories, she knows where each box and crate should go, and when the time comes to send stock out to the markets, she knows what is needed and where. Without her, the markets would barely work. There would be chaos.

And of course I love her, beyond all reason; but I have never told her that, and that is something I regret, because now I never will. So please, say nothing, to anyone.

*

The Walkers are Machinist Tippit's. We know him.

"New stock," he says, taking a glass tube of documents from a pouch in his suit and handing it to me. He won't hand it to Hypatia; he never does.

We have never seen Machinist Tippit's face. We have never seen what hides behind the stitched leather mask, or the obsidian darkness of the eyeshieldings; even his gait seems hidden beneath the recesses and tubing of the hermetically sealed suit he wears.

I open the tube.

"Fire Feeders," he says, before I have a chance to begin reading. "There have been new developments with fire." His voice has taken on a new tone; hubris, I think it is called. I do not like it.

Workers, strapped into clanking and hissing lifters, are already unloading crates of the new devices from the Walkers' dark holds.

"All instances of fire will now require one of these. *All* instances…" — he pauses briefly — "New developments with fire," he repeats pointlessly.

Hypatia reaches into a crate and retrieves a cylinder of tinted glass, apparently empty, and mounted in a framework of brass piping and tubes, from which extends an array of knobs, keys, and valves.

There is no sound as she moves, her tattooed skin slides easily among the prosthetics. Her machinery moves with practiced, easy precision. Her eyepiece clicks almost imperceptibly as she studies the device.

"Machinist Tippit, on whose authori…?"

"The Council of Cardinals," he interrupts her. The Machinist hides neither his impatience nor his disdain. He does not like the Serapeum, and he does not like us. "Every instance of fire, whether industrial or domestic, must be fed the output from Valves Two, Four, and Subletting Valve D, which must be engaged concomitantly with the Release Control Activator and the Filter Engagement at Locus Two. We…" — he gestures with a gloved hand, in such a way that it is clear that he is referring to himself in particular — "…will be adding Fire Infringements to the list of Surveillable Activities and Warrantable Exigencies. In short, Librarian, every fire will require a Fire Feeder." He pauses, for a rasping breath. "And your… establishment, of course, will distribute them."

"I see. New developments with fire, indeed." Hypatia hands the device to him, smiles as he hesitates before reaching to take it. Even through his mask and suit, his discomfort at the thought of physical contact with her is palpable. "No doubt this has all been well thought out. Good day, Machinist." She turns to me. "Come, Synesius."

As she turns to leave, Hypatia gives me the look that I have seen before; the one that means — *there is more to say,* and — *but not here* and — *oh, who are these clowns?* and — *be careful* … all somehow rolled into one.

You might think that she could be staid, or too studious (do they mean the same thing? I would have to ask her, that's the sort of thing she knows without having to open a book or a scroll), or perhaps she might be quiet, or even dour. She is a Head Librarian, after all, so none of these would be a surprise, would they?

But none of this is the case. She has a raw, untrammelled, this-is-what-it-is intelligence. Like a zebra, she cannot be tamed. She applies her mind to whatever she chooses, with an enthusiasm that, I know, some see as wanton. She disturbs some people, makes them uneasy.

She does this: she traces and records the paths that the birds draw in the sky and the creening of the fish in the streams at night, and the height of the Silverkros flower stalks after three days of rain, and the rhythm of cloven hooves, which when enumerated, makes her heart thrill — and she says that there are *so* many ideas and facts, and things that might *just* be facts, that sometimes she feels as though her mind is going to explode in a wonderful kaleidoscope of thoughts, and each thought is a flame, or a spark, and it's like a huge, endless orgasm of stars, and thinking, and wonder, and gratitude, and love for it all, and amazement that it can be so deep and clear, and full of light, and steal your breath without trying at all, or really doing anything, and she laughs and says *that's* what thinking is, and *that's* what science is, *and* what love is, and it's all one thing; and there's no difference between any of it.

So. I can't argue, can I? I just say yes.

*

"I do not trust the Machinists, Synesius."

I know. I say nothing. Pathetically, I hope that my silence will encourage hers. Things are complicated enough already; but she continues.

"And I do not like these Fire Feeder things. There is something wrong."

Of that, I am not so sure. Their reasons may be obscure

at times, but the rule of the Cardinals gives us order. They keep us all fed, they keep the Markets full. They have allowed the Library to exist; the Theological Office pays many of our expenses. And the people have their Amulets and their Soil Conditioners and their Filters — all at the behest of the Cardinals. So yes, I am unsure.

"I am going to look into this." Hypatia's eyes ripple with anticipation. She writes a note on her arm, on the square of bare skin — often used for this purpose — just beside the hasp of her left elbow assembly. When she writes there, it is always something that she will get to very soon.

I finally accept that I must say something.

"I will be busy, cataloguing the soil samples from the farms," I say. "Perhaps I will help you later," I add, intending, but failing, to lie.

*

I go to the Market sometimes, when I need time and space to think. I know there's some sort of paradox there. The Market is crowded, full of noise and chaos. Despite being at the foot of the cliff face that the Library dominates, and therefore close enough for the two to be considered parts of a whole, it always feels like a world apart.

Everything in the Library feels so important, but in the Market there are so many things to do without, and it all feels so *un*important. Oh… it's not worth getting complicated about… I come here to think, that's all.

They have been selling the Fire Feeders here for a month now. A stern-faced Fiscal Probity Marshall from the District Planning College has given the stallholders who qualify the requisite paperwork and certificates; she has collected the Onsellers' Fees and License Application Bonds, and has seen that the Market Committee's *Undertaking to Accept*

Responsibilities Charter has been amended, cited, ratified (twice), and signed.

Pending approval by the Inspectors from the Planning College and countersigning by the Theological Office, everything is in order. The stallholders will soon be able to make formal applications for permanent licenses.

As always, Croesus the Lydian is there, with his piles of Magnesium Amulets (for the pig farmers) and Fertility Harmonic Essentials (for the croppers, and for domestic use); and his collection of Conditioners and Filters, of course. Since the Planning College ended the sale of real food at the Markets, traders like Croesus have done well.

Masked though he is, I recognise him by his modifications. He wears the crudely articulated but well-sealed suit of a Trader, not all that different from the suits worn by Farmers and Labourers. The corrugated leather outer skin and pneumatic tubing protects him from the air, and the heaviest eyeshieldings available protect his sight from constant exposure to the glare of the sun. All going well, he will not be blind for some years yet.

"Synesius! Look at this…" Croesus holds up one of the new Feeders.

"Yes, I know. I've seen them."

Croesus grunts. "These things… look what they're telling us…"

He hands me a sheet. Yes, I've seen this before, as well. But I stand there, and I read it again. The Cardinals have taken scientific advice to the effect that raw fire is destructive to the air; that for the sake of the common good, and so that the air is not consumed and so that all life on the earth does not perish, if not *very* soon then at least *soon*, and if not *soon* then within a few short generations, and do you not care about your children, and what sort of world are we going to leave for future generations?... and so on, and so on, then on account of all those things, and for the common good, the Council of Cardinals has decreed that all fire must be accompanied by a Fire Feeder, and that any case of fire being unattended by a Fire Feeder is most deleterious in its effect on the common good, and will be dealt with appropriately — which is to say, harshly.

All this said, the sheet finishes with the admonition that the Machinists will police the new regulations vigorously.

I had forgotten about all this. Or I had tried. Hypatia has seemed preoccupied for the last week, and I know it has to with these accursed cylinders. Her work has suffered, and her mood has changed. The notes that she has been writing on her clothes and skin have been taking on a different tone, one that I haven't seen before, and on several occasions, she has even hidden them from my sight.

I sigh. I know Croesus, I know that he will have something more for me. "Alright, my friend. Tell me..."

It is easier for him to take me to his village.

*

"This," he says, as he shows me an iron smelter with furnaces that are cold and silent. "They cannot afford the fees, nor the Scribe to complete the forms."

"And this," as he opens the door of a farmer's hut, and someone hurries to hide an illegal flame. "They do not qualify."

"And here." A seed winnower has left a week's work behind, to go to prison because of unpaid debt. His yard is in disarray. "His family will wait for a time, and then they will despair, and then they will go, and the last of the seed will disappear into the wind."

"Tell him, Croesus," the villagers say, when they see the insignia of the Library on my suit. "Show him the ruined food, the empty purses, animals and children gone hungry for fear of the Walkers who come stalking fearsomely out of the mist, how we struggle to share one Fire Feeder between too many hearths… We were poor before, and now look at us… At least we have our faith, and our amulets…"

I have seen enough. "These things are the ruin of these people," I say.

"You have it, my friend," Croesus replies. "There was a time when I would happily have made money by selling toys and trinkets to these people, but no more, Synesius. I have done this for long enough."

*

When I return, Hypatia is in her laboratory. Something I almost recognise is being dismantled, sprawled across a table, a collapsed cage of tubes, clockwork, and instruments.

"Librarian. I will help you."

She barely looks up, but I do see a smile. "At last. Now, take this. And this. Dismantle them. See whether they match. Whether they can serve a common purpose, or whether they are specific to the tasks which they apparently perform. And then put them back together. Please."

And soon I know what she has been doing, and that she has been right all along.

*

She has explained everything. It is among her best work, I am sure. The rest of us post copies of it on doors and walls in the villages, hand them out at the Market below the Serapeum and at all the other markets — as far as we can reach.

Soon everyone knows what she has discovered; that the

Fire Feeders do nothing. They are useless, inert, their parts are not internally connected in any way that serves a function. Everything about them and of them and in them is for show, and does precisely nothing.

Hypatia presents her findings in words and pictures and supports her case using anecdotes, comparisons, metaphors and similes. The point can escape no one; the argument is undeniable. The word spreads through the markets, and beyond, to the villages and farms, to the other libraries, to the large cities... Soon, the news has travelled everywhere, and soon after that, no one is buying Fire Feeders any more.

Crowds gather and burn their Certificates and Permissions and Notices of Allocation on fires lit, pointedly and loudly, without the aid of Fire Feeders. Feeders are broken and trampled and thrown at the officers from the Planning College, and then at their Walkers as they retreat, shamed, unratified, and penniless.

The priests from the Theological Office watch, conferring in low, troubled voices.

I am concerned. "This could get out of control," I say to Hypatia.

She smiles. "A free mind cannot be commanded, Synesius. Let the people discover their freedom, it is time that these traces were thrown off."

But I can see that Hypatia has noticed the men from the Theological Office, and I have noticed them, and they have noticed us. The air is thick with noticing.

*

"How pleasant, another visit," — but Machinist Tippit is having none of such niceties.

"You are responsible, and you will stop it," he rasps. His anger! You can hear his outrage seething behind his mask.

It is a tense moment; he has not come alone.

Whatever his intention, it doesn't work. The pleading (which is disguised); the threats and blustering (not so disguised). None of it works. He even tries —

"... and they nurse their ignorance, Librarian; they've grown to *like* their sores so much that they scratch them to keep them festering. Words are no use. Only the force and violence of being ruled over absolutely, to the core of their being, makes any sense to them..."

"Free minds, Machinist," says Hypatia, looking through the window at the perfect circle of the moon, as though that in itself might be enough, and he will understand.

Machinist Tippit says nothing, but my fear is that he *does* understand, or that if he does not, then his Cardinals will.

*

So. Machinist Tippit's report to the Cardinals must have been delivered.

There is violence now. The supporters of the Cardinals have appeared, and they swarm like black ants, and there seem to be so *many*. They burn and strike and attack, and they are aided by Machinists, who pour out of Walkers everywhere.

They are at the gates of the Library, and now they have pushed their way through, and people are wounded and calling for help, but there is none to be had; there is fighting, and there are flames, and now there are dead, and the statues of the gods are falling and crumbling... *Serapis, save yourself...*

There is fighting everywhere now. She knows what I am thinking.

"Everything flowers, Synesius. All entelechies unfold, according to their natures. Yours. Mine. Theirs. That is all there is."

The gears in her arms whir as she passes the works of the Philosopher to me. "Get these to safety, Synesius," her voice clicks.

The noise of the crowd draws closer. She seems to notice that her skin is covered with writing. "And this must go," she says, and turns towards her rooms.

Buildings burn through the night. The Serapeum's books and scrolls lie disintegrated in drifts of flame and smoke and ashes. Machinists trample through the fires, heedless of the heat, pouring fuel on the flames.

In just a few hours, a thousand years is dust and ash.

*

The next morning, Walkers beyond counting stream out of the early morning gloom into the towns and villages, through the smoking ruins of the Library and what remains of the Market, coughing clouds of searing gas, loudspeakers blaring:

The air is in danger of dying. Renegades have been burning fires without permission and without the requisite devices in attendance. We are spraying remediant to counter the imminent danger of environmental collapse. Despite the irritation to your lungs, please breathe as deeply as possible. What sort of world do you want to leave for coming generations?

The sky darkens. The sun is hidden behind a mass that suddenly hangs over everything. I have seen engravings of what is above us, so I know what it is. But still, to actually *see* one...

It is a *bolo* airship, so large that its prow and stern seem to disappear into the haze of the distance.

The Cardinals are here.

*

There are many of us, herded into a hall aboard the *bolo*. I have been taken too, but I am not in chains; I am not being tried before the Council of Cardinals. It is even whispered that if I am careful, I have a future. I am saying nothing.

Hypatia was among the first taken. She stands chained, upright, and she meets their gaze without faltering. I doubt that I have ever loved her as much as I do right now. What follows achieves nothing.

—*So you are the wheel, are you?* Hypatia says to them, and they do not understand, but I do, because I have seen the butterfly tattooed on the curve of her back.

—*I think that the ocean is deep enough,* she says later, and again they do not understand, but again I do, and I am not surprised that she says nothing more to them after that, and that there are no tears when they command the Machinists to come and tie her to the rack on which she will now surely die.

There is some sort of ceremony. I don't know. They pronounce something, observe some sort of outer form, I don't know.

I realise now that I have been waiting for this moment, anticipating it so much that I feel an awful relief now that it is finally here. From now on, everything that moves, everything that is thought — everything — they all link up, the pieces of everything roar like the wind as they come together, like the cogs in a machine that has no way of stopping.

I can barely hear. There are no individual sounds, there is only one sound, and it is immense, an impenetrable wall that obscures everything.

The inevitability of it shudders in my mind. Is this vengeance, or a lesson for the masses? The hall is crowded.

The names of the things that I see have dissolved; the performance I am watching is beyond names. The Cardinals gather around, and insist that I stand with them. I would look at the floor, but I cannot. The floor has dissolved as well.

Machinists, Tippit among them, with knives and saws and screwdrivers and tools — too small and delicate to determine their names or uses with any certainty — surround Hypatia, and begin to dismantle her.

"I suspected by the look of him that he enjoys killing things," she says to me, looking up at Tippit as he removes her arms, unscrewing and cutting, cursing, but not impatiently, as her blood soaks into his instruments. She bites her lip, her eyes close for a second, and then open again.

"Does it hurt?" I ask, hopelessly. I can think of nothing else to say.

"The pain is breathtaking," she replies, as a saw begins to open her chest. "Space and time, they are mere irritants, Synesius," — but it is harder to understand her now, because her mouth fills with bloody foam as she speaks.

A Machinist begins to remove wire from her chest cavity.

"Aah, the heart…!", and the Cardinals gather around, "let us see the heart!" and there is glee among them.

"What can I do?" I whisper.

And there is a glance that will cut me in half forever, and then the light in her eyes has gone out.

And I cannot see Hypatia, and I cannot recognise the things and pieces that were her, nor the Machinists, who are still cutting and pulling and excising, nor the Cardinals, who are full of joy and happiness — they are all just parts, and pieces, and their names have all gone.

And as these things fall away, dripping into the dust where her blood gathers — there I can almost recognise what I thought to be me, the thing that gave names to the world, and I see now, quite clearly, that there is nothing there either.

*

The flesh which three times I touched is gone. It has been ground with seashells, and fed to the dogs.

In the end, the Cardinals were full of joy at the death.

They had been surprised when there was no heart to be found inside her. There were organs, true, and blood, true, and cogs and gears and devices of exotic and wonderful manufacture — but there was no heart.

They wondered at this, but only briefly. Then they ordered the flesh disposed of, and the mechanical parts cleaned of blood and gore, and sent to the factories, to be used there, assimilated into the machines that make the Amulets and Feeders and Filters and Conditioners.

"This will make things easier," said the Cardinals. "Our production values will be greatly enhanced. Going forward, we expect positive impacts on Liquidity and Market Penetration. Stability has returned!"

*

But *I* know where her heart is; I think I have known all along. Her heart was in the ease and effortless power of her machinery, it was in the heat and pulse of her flesh, and the way the rhythms of them both flowed from the one to the other, and from the other to the one, in the way it all found form in her thinking, and science, and love — there was never any difference between any of them...

And every idea that she had, the urging of every thought towards the freedom of her mind and her spirit — they all left their mark, an imprint of her intent, her joy, in every cog, every gear, every piece of brass and obsidian; they were *all* her; there was no difference between any of them...

And now, do you see it?

She is everywhere, taken and installed in the machinery of their factories, where the production lines create one thing after another, charm after charm, device after device, again and again without end, every one with Hypatia in them, *imago*, complete and perfect, imprinted not just in their form but in their essence, in the habits that form them, and from there they go out to the world, delivered by hordes of Walkers to markets and libraries everywhere, where one day — yes, one day — there will be enough...

*

So, there you have it. There is your answer. That is what happened concerning the pagan Hypatia. Now please, say nothing of this.

THE PRINCESS ASLAUGA

A FAIRY TALE FROM THE CLOCK

THERE WAS ONCE A GIRL — excuse me, a young woman, you decide — who on account of having no excuse at all for an episode of bad behaviour, bad language, and bad attitude, was sent to her room. Not *straight* to her room, which is to say, without dinner, because none of the behaviour, language, or attitude were irredeemably atrocious or outrageous — but the whole package, considered together, was of the type about which grown-ups eventually, and quite rightfully, come to the conclusion that they have just had enough.

And this was behaviour which really could not be ignored; there would be a cleaning bill to countenance, and apologies to make, and eyes to roll during the retelling, and so the girl was given over to the servants. And before the jugglers and the clowns and the singers, and even the dancing Syrians (who said they were Sufis, but who could be sure?), had begun — before in fact, *any* of the King's birthday celebrations had begun; as soon as the fruit pureed with ice from the peaks of the Urals and dusted with honeyed pollen brushed from the wings of Baalbek doves had been served — yes, dinner having been done, the miscreant was sent to her room.

Now, you are curious as to the nature of the trouble, I know. I can hear your restlessness from here; it reminds me of the way the archers from the palace guard grumble as they practice in the courtyard early on a cold morning, far below my window. But I am not going to tell you; not because I don't want to, particularly — you see, I have no agenda and can be trusted implicitly — but because she and I, we have made a deal, and a good deal it is; in exchange for my silence on certain matters, and the reasons for the transgressions of the evening in question are the least of them (and I must admit that too much education of some people can be just as injurious as too little or none at all; so I am being careful about what I tell you — but please don't take offence; I mean none of this personally) — I have been told that I can tell you the following.

*

The next day, she sought me out, while the mead hall was being returned to its normal immaculate state after the King's birthday celebrations, which had apparently gone on all night, and were fit to keep even the monsters in their lairs on the marshes awake and grumbling — but let us not get started on monsters, for if we do that, we shall be here indefinitely...

The child (and I persist in thinking of her as a child; I think because of my own age, and the difference between us, rather than just her youth, which in itself is just a thing, and of no great importance; but also because if my own daughter had lived, she would be of the same order of age as the Princess; perhaps that has something to do with it, as well...) ...the child, as I say... pressed upon me that I should put down my bucket and mop and follow her, so I did, because of course you do not refuse the Princess; none of us would ever think of it, and so I followed the Princess, and she led me — and do I need to describe my consternation, the ice which wrapped itself around my heart, the tightening of my lips, so that for several moments no words could part them, when I saw that she had led me to the door, heavy with chains and locks, shut fast with dire warnings and old rumours, sealed with whispers and averted eyes — you know of course, which door; I refer to *that* door, huge and unused for so long — she had led me to the room that had been sealed for as many years as the Princess is old (and you shall see how that works).

The tapestry that had concealed it since the day of the young Princess's arrival lay in a convulsed pile on the floor where she had dropped it sometime during the night, when she should have been sleeping, and the guard outside her room should not; a mountain and attending foothills of brocaded skies and forest, and nymphs and satyrs, and a huge naked Artemis, lying sprawled and wanton across the floor.

'I would have that door opened,' said the Princess, turning to me rather than anyone else, her head held straight and her gaze clearer than that of anyone who had attended the King's celebrations — and addressing me rather than anyone else. Of course. I always seem to get these jobs.

*

Now, please be patient; I need to digress. I have erred. With my mention of King's birthdays, and jugglers, and being sent to rooms, and the dinner being exotic (Baalbek doves, *really?*), I think that quite possibly I have created in your mind a picture of the King as a sort of avuncular character, perhaps with a jolly smile, rosy cheeks, a happy and knowing twinkle in his eye — think of Saint Nicholas if you must — and perhaps a Queen beside him, beautiful and wise and radiant, a good mother to the royal household and the realm; and you probably had thought, if you dwelt on the matter at all, that you have not met these two yet simply because I have yet to introduce you.

And you may have an image in your mind of the young Princess as being a very young child, of maybe ten or eleven, which of course is the age at which all children are precocious and heartless, and I did mention some bad behaviour, after all, and young girls combine these traits with a terrible lack of mercy, as thoroughly and as skilfully as the cooks in hell's kitchens, where of course the meal and the diner are often one and the same; a condition well-known to all parents.

Oh my, is that what you were thinking? We have gone a little distance down the wrong track, haven't we... children do that to us, don't they? One minute we're sure of what we know, and then just one child, one sweet Princess later, we find, out of nowhere, a shock, like stepping into autumn leaves and finding a drain or a gutter lurking beneath, and there goes your ankle; or having killed the dragon and taken the treasure, slipping on the blood-slippery stone at the entrance of the creature's lair, because you were not watching your step, and were thinking ahead too hard, too far, already dividing the jewels and gold and pearls between the members of your family, and so you slipped on the shed life blood of the dead monster (perhaps you were distracted by the mournful cry of its mother, perhaps the revenge that she swore to the heavens, causing the sea to boil, made you blanch a little, and miss your step...), and you lost your grip on the jewellery, the gold, the pearls, because you had to reach out, in a panic, and take hold of something, anything — a handhold of rock, or the branch of a blackened, scorched tree — to stop you and your armour and your horse and your servants and your supply wagons and your guards all from crashing, head over heel, one over the other, over and over, around and round, down over the precipice, into the abyss over which the dragon had kept guard, keeping the foolish and unwise away, so they should not dash their brains out on the rocks — and so you could do nothing but watch, your balance recovered but still precarious, as the treasure tumbled into the depths, and crashed to the bottom of the very pit from which the monster had first retrieved it. If you had not been distracted by the treasure, you would not have lost the treasure.

Hmm. Perhaps this is what tales of young royals do. Yes, I have digressed, and more than I intended to.

In short — yes, you see, I *can* do it, I *can* be brief — the Princess is: reserved, aloof, often withdrawn, introspective, frequently accused of rudeness or surliness, attractive, wide-eyed, not given to suffering fools, well-read, sometimes irascible (though never without cause), seventeen, raven-haired, intelligent (although so uninterested in the astrolabe that she has never touched one), given to gazing at the moon and composing verse which she never writes down, and of course, she is not the natural daughter of the King or Queen, and therefore lacks both the King's raptorial nature and the Queen's proclivity for screaming at anything or anyone, regardless of their distance from her, or their degree of fault in the matter at hand;

— and here is the King of Norway — he is short, and I don't need to tell you, of all people, how little is the trust that should be placed in short men, because they hate the world so much on account of its ruthlessness and its enjoyment in seeing them cuckolded; and he is thin, and you must never trust those who are thin, because they are always hungry; and he is old, and so many of the old care about all the wrong things, or nothing — or even worse, about nothing so much as soft food.

The King is harsh, and careless, and cruel. Yet do not think that he is unfeeling; for he feels everything, and he finds much relief and satisfaction in the pain of those he delivers it to;

— and now you're wondering how the Queen fits in.

She fits in like this: where he is short, she is not (she towers above him); where he speaks but little, she is an endless torrent of words; where he is cruel — well, she *is* that. The King loves the Queen — to the degree and in the manner that he does — simply because he cannot cause her pain, and this impresses him greatly; in fact the delirium of it often deprives him of sleep. She is impervious to him. Between them, in public as well as in private, they have established this beyond all doubt, with a certainty and thoroughness that would cause some to descend to the outer regions of madness. (Their relationship is not alone in this; but it is a good example of it.)

The King and the Queen preside over their realm as though no one else could possibly do it, or has ever done it before them. Only the mountains and the rocks and trees and the rivers and lakes, and the winds that hunt and race above it all, and the hamadryads that live in all of it, can remember the time when the King's predecessor sat on the throne — but he was a fool, and quick enough about dying; and so they keep their silence, because for everything that exists, there is something for which a dagger can serve as a metaphor, along the blade of which glistens doom and dissolution.

Now in the days surrounding these events, the realm has come to resemble the Royal Couple; Norway has taken after them, just as any child will its parents eventually, through either imitation or resentment. (The effect, though often understandably unpopular, is inescapable and inevitable.)

Accordingly, the rivers here do not begin life as babbling brooks, all sparkling happiness and innocence; that is for the weak who live in the south, where it is warm, where the ice does not reach, where the heat saps strength, and the sun bleaches souls.

No, here the mountains are made of the same fury that possesses the King and the Queen, and just as it does with them, it causes the very earth to shake, so that from the mountains erupt cascades of lust and febrility, of rigour and will, as water that boils, but not on account of its temperature; as mist that rises not because it is steam, but because it rises to challenge the hot blood of the housecarls and the crews of the dragon-prowed longboats, and tests them, and then sooths their brows when they prove themselves strong and resolute;

and the water coursing through the rivers and streams is the relentless lifeblood of the world, bearing within it memories of strength and war and regret for nothing;

as waterfalls, it hurls itself into the frozen northern air, fearless, careless, and the men and women who breathe in the sight feel no doubt or fear, and the broadsword and the shield of the housecarl house its strength without fail or hesitation;

and it flows to the sea, and its memory does not dissolve there, but retains itself, like the recollection of a great victory of arms, and it picks up the dragon-prowed longboats and carries them across the broad ocean, to the southern lands of the soft and weak, whose mourning and doom is written on the blades of northern swords.

And the King and Queen preside over all this, and neither of them care anything for weakness, or failure, or children.

*

Oh yes, the door. We were in front of the door, weren't we…

We stood, the young Princess and her friends and retainers, unmoving like so much *terra cotta*, before the door, the age and silence of which left heavy weights upon our tongues; the slow, effortless rusting of the iron frame reminded me of the dust-covered bark of the forests of Finland, captured in luxuriant, faithful fashion by the King's court painter, in the memorials that hang in the summer banquet hall and in which the blood of the fallen depicted on the snow glows fierce and red when the light of the morning sun streams in, a flood of pale heat through high-arched windows, turning everything golden and red; but this is the heavy red of languid slow desire, the red that lowers eyelids and averts the gaze, that sends mouths fleeing to hide behind fans of burgundy lace, that puts an edge on the intake of a breath when a hand touches or brushes — or a glance brushes or lingers — or a gesture lingers or rests; and beneath it all courses an endless, red, stream of blood and deep, unending appetite.

The door was soon opened, of course.

*

And soon we were standing on the very spot upon which I had stood all those years ago, with the King and Queen there as well, standing at the edge of the water that filled the room; the gaping hole as wide as a dragon-prowed longship is long, filled with water into the depths of which there is no seeing; they and the members of the court, the lords and ladies and courtesans and sycophants and hangers-on, they were all there, but no-one knew anything as to what this was; but somehow it promised some great change, or at least the chance of it.

I can tell you, because I was there.

The room in which the royal court and its hangers-on stood had been uncovered during renovations in preparation for the birth of the Queen's child; it had by all appearances been built around the edifice of the well, which had itself, by all appearances, been built by unknown hands, a long age ago, around the body of water. The water was dark and timeless and reeked of mystery and inscrutability, and had clearly itself been built around nothing; even a Saxon or a Russian, or a Dane such as I, could tell *that* much…

Some of us shook or shivered with fright; some of us could not look upon the water; some could not take their eyes from it. I cannot remember where I stood among all that.

It was the only time I have ever seen the King unsure, or the Queen unable to speak. (As for the singular nature of *that* circumstance, please just accept the notion without further discussion, otherwise we shall be here all day.)

But more than just water was at the root of the unease. Do you remember what I said about the power that resides in the water here, and how these people were so used to it? A power that broods or rages in water is nothing new. It would take more than a bottomless pool of water to gather a crowd here.

Before us, insensible and impervious to our dismay, and bobbing slightly on the water as a toy boat might after its owner has been distracted by the flurry of a flock of crimson parrots flying from a copse of trees — was a thing of wood and brass. It resembled a turtle as much as it resembled anything; or a wooden egg embraced by metallic limbs as much as it resembled anything else.

Water slickened its surfaces of dark and polished wood; water dripped from its handles and propellers, dripped from its raised hatch surrounded by portholes all made of brass and from which a mist of light glowed, causing the wetness on it to shine and shimmer, as though somewhere, within the space that this apparition occupied, with all its strangeness and wood and brass, a sun had risen, so that fingers of dawn pierced the gloom like rose thorns, and crimson parrots flew close, and somewhere there were marks of teeth on skin...

Now the Queen had, a few weeks before, lost the child that she had been carrying. It was not greatly developed, she not being far into the pregnancy; and the people in question being who they were, there were no tears or histrionics, and both the physical and elemental qualities of the landscape being what they were, no rivers had reversed their directions, nor had there been any eclipse or earthquake, nor had any statues turned, toppled, or wept. In fact, the truth of it is that the death of the unborn child had been forgotten almost instantly; make of that what you will. As for myself and the other prisoners, we did not look the matter in the eye, we just continued with our work, covering ourselves in the silence which all in our situation embrace, if they have any wisdom at all.

But on that morning, as the King and Queen and their attendants gathered in this strange room, the matter of children must surely have surfaced in their minds — because from the strange and barnacle-encrusted construction which floated before them, from the portholes of which a soft glow of light emanated, and the hatch of which had opened, they were told, by itself — the sound of a child happily burbling could plainly be heard.

In short, there was an infant in this thing, this diving machine which had risen from the depths of the black water just an hour before, in the full and shocked presence of workers, who, being superstitious, illiterate and uneducated (which is to say, foreigners), had dropped their tools and fled at the sight of the monster as it had heaved above the surface of the water, hissing, its gears winding down noisily as it came to rest.

The workers had informed their overseer, who had come and looked, and then had left and informed *his* overseer, who had come and looked... and so on and so on, and soon there had been so much coming and looking and overseeing going on that the King and the Queen found themselves standing before the machine, listening to the sound of what was irrefutably an increasingly hungry human infant.

It wasn't long before the child had been retrieved from the vessel. The process involved two Danish prisoners, an English courtesan, and a Norwegian guard, himself not long released from prison, where he had spent a few months atoning for his practice of *trolldomr* — a tallying by which he was not one bit deterred.

Seeing the looks of wonder on the faces of the onlookers, the Queen stepped forward, took the baby from the Englishwoman, and said, as if it were the end of the matter and would resolve all doubts or complications or speculation: "The Princess Aslauga."

The King nodded deliberately, this signifying that he was not about to interfere, even though, as was often the case in matters concerning the Queen, he had no idea of what was happening.

And that was that.

The Princess grew up as the daughter of the King and Queen, and no-one ever told her any differently.

Which is why it is something of a mystery; how she came

to know of the door which had been concealed from her and the world for so long, and so well. I have my suspicions, but because they do not involve people talking, or people being told, or secrets being betrayed, or whispers, or notes, then I think that I shall not tell you, because if you are like most people, you would not believe me. Me, who has no agenda.

But all that was then, a long time ago.

*

Here we were, again.

The Princess and I stood before the water, which was exactly as we had left it all those years ago — just as dark and impenetrable as when the door was sealed. Also exactly as we had left it was the diving vessel.

The Princess had sent the others away, and the two of us stood in the pale light of the winter sun struggling through the dust-encrusted windows high above us, washing the color from everything, so that she, and I know I must have as well, took on the appearance of a ghost, standing there, the shade of a smile haunting her pale lips.

'I will enter the bell, Bernardo,' she said, using my Danish name, rather than that Norwegian slur they use to degrade me, and which I shall not mention here.

And she did enter the bell, and I helped her.

She waited until I had returned to what this strange room provided by way of a shore — this involved some lowering and raising of walkways — and then she closed the hatch of the bell, as she called it; and indeed, there was something of a ringing sound as it was shut up.

Then pieces of the device began to move, as though some train of events had been set in motion, which it most clearly was, as you shall see.

So as for what happened next, I cannot tell from having seen it myself, but I *do* have it from her own lips, and I can assure you that her account is to be trusted, for of all the people in this castle, the Princess Aslauga is the one who is truthful to her core, in whose heart there is no crevice or flaw in which the angel of deceit might find a foothold (I think it has to do with her provenance) — so, if she says that this is how it happened, then yes, this is how it happened...

*

The Princess descends into the water, past the point where I can no longer see the bell because darkness has swallowed it, and the sound of it, the ticking and grinding of its gears and the hiss of something that I do not understand has ceased, and I stand there and look, feeling helpless now, at the only trace of what has just happened. The settling disturbance of the water. The eddies of pale reflections...

As the bell takes her into the black depths, light spills from its portholes and illuminates the creatures that live here. Her breath gasps first, and then her heart and her mind gasp as well. The creatures here are so many and so fearsome; out of the darkness they swim towards her, they bare their teeth, huge and curved like the sabres of the King's housecarls. Some brush their hoary scales against the side of the bell, and the sound of that is like names to her, heady names of things that want to take form and that almost make her swoon.

Crystals of ice form on the windows, and her flesh thrills with the cold as she wipes them away, so that she can see out to where the light dispels the darkness and reveals great hides and long, scaled backs. Eyes the size of cart wheels gaze back at her. She has said nothing. She says nothing.

And then past a great tear, a fissure in the water; through which, illuminated by a sun which never sets or eclipses, and which calls for no blood or sacrifice, she sees a great open field on which a godchild plays endless games with tortoises and kangaroos and lizards and Silent Gray Ibolons from the desert worlds of N53-157; all of these playmates being infinite in number, and seven light years long, except for the Ibolons, which are *especially* large;

From there the Princess travels down through the freezing sea, to where the creatures become thin and insubstantial and far apart, and they float like sheets of gossamer and forget first each others' names and then their own;

And past the male and female gods and deities, past even the very point where the Goddess is enveloping the God, and He is entering Her, past the point where all their arms are intertwined in love, and all their bodies and legs are intertwined in love, so that Aslauga blushes, for prudence and on account of the sight of others, but also for eagerness and desire...

And she arrives, her craft in perfect repair, despite the pressures of the deep which would collapse the world to the size of a pinprick, if only the world could survive there long enough for that to happen; the weight of the water here is infinite; yet every piece and cog and gear of the bell is still functioning.

Here she is, at the place where the things that exist slide up against the things that do not exist, and they whisper together on the ocean floor.

The Princess navigates the bell to a place where existence and non-existence slide over each other like lovers, and she feels herself flicker, most deliciously and agreeably, and she smiles at the joy of this, because it is very deep down here, and not many bother to attempt the journey, and even fewer make it to the plane where existence and non-existence meet, where they do indeed (yes, she sees that now) slide over each other like sweat-soaked lovers, and the Princess smiles because she sees a great whale in the impeccable half-light of the distance, swimming near a ridge of doubt and curiosity, and a pool of light paints pictures on the eyes of the beast, and on its great hide are scars which are shaped like words such as might be in a book, if only books could contain words that large, or even if books could just exist down here, but then they cannot — and so she feels thankful that whales can. If only she had paid more attention to her books and her reading, especially the volumes on whales!

And then her smile becomes wide, and she laughs with such joy that all the deities and creatures come diving and flying to see, and far above the God and the Goddess hear her, and pause, and lift their teeth from each others' skin, and look into each others' eyes, She into His and He into Hers, and they laugh, and create several new universes, one of which, reader, is the one you are sitting in right now.

*

So I was told. The Princess Aslauga returned to us in the same manner that she had left, with the bell rising from the depths noisily, with much clanking and whirring and cascading water. And although she swore it was only a few minutes, it was a week that she was gone.

She has never been the same since. And now sometimes she disappears, for days at a time, and I know where she is, of course. Her secret is safe with me, for I have no agenda, and can be trusted implicitly. And every time she comes out of that room, I see that she has grown more, and says less, and every day she looks at the Moon, or where the Moon would be if it was there, and she composes verses, but she does not write them down.

But she does tell them to me, and as for that; perhaps another time.

THE TOWER

I HAVE BEEN TOLD that we have been building this tower for thousands of years.

I have no direct experience; no reason to believe this — nor to doubt it — but it is what I have heard, and I can see a little way into the waters that keep rising, lapping below our feet as we keep building, board after board, nail after nail.

In the depths, dissolving into the darkness that is the limit of our vision, the faint shapes of the bulwarks that my predecessors built in defiance of the water linger — but they failed; I can see also the remnants of the sealed chambers, broken, flooded and empty, the seals torn and perished. Nothing has worked; the waters still rise, taking everything out of reach; it all becomes illusion and memory.

The Enemy who lives in the water comes without warning; I think he never really departs, he just lurks out of sight, waiting. The Enemy is clever, I think; he changes his shape from one minute to the other, but his shadow is always the same.

We build upward — spar by spar, a piece of wall here, so that we know where one room stops and the next begins, a piece of ceiling there, which will become tomorrow's floor; ever upward. Sometimes it is tiring, but sometimes, too, it is exhilarating. On those days we have so much hope, and it is good to build, and we are sure then that when everything is said and done, as one day it surely must be, the Tower, somehow, will love us for our work, or at least will approve of it, and our hope will be vindicated — and what is hope for, if not for vindication?

I hear them being taken, sometimes, the others, while they are working in the next room, or a few rooms down a hallway, or across a square, or off a thoroughfare (for the Tower is very, very large...).

Sometimes, when the Enemy takes one of us, he is quiet about it; they do not struggle or shout; I suppose he must come looming up out of the darkness before they can do anything — or perhaps before they even know he is there, or upon them; he must lay his grasp around their hearts, and flood through them, and there is no mercy; and they are gone without a sound, as if they were never awake.

But I do not really know; I have never seen it. I have only heard about it.

And then there are other times, when the Enemy comes roaring, as a great noise like a wind that wants to tear everything apart, and throw us over, our work and all, down into the water together, and to circle above us, whipping waves into knives that rend us into small pieces that no longer know each other. At those times, there can be a great panic that spreads, and everything is so huge, and those who the Enemy has taken into his cold embrace cry, and I have heard them begging, but the Enemy is implacable.

Sometimes he throws them around like dolls, breaking them, sending them down to their destruction, where we cannot see. But I do not really know; I have never seen it.

Sometimes, the Tower shakes, the Enemy is so strong.

But we keep building, although we never draw away from the water; it keeps rising with us, always just below our feet, rising as we build, but just beyond our reach; so that even if we lie down, in a place where we might be about to place a floorboard, or where we might have lifted one up; pulled the nails, and prised it away (although this is frowned upon, and is not regarded as contributing to the building of the Tower; so it is not often done, or at least admitted to) — though we might lie flat and extend our arms, straining as hard as we can, or relax them, until they are like the water itself, we cannot ever reach the water. No-one, to tell you the truth, even knows what it feels like; there are all sorts of stories about it.

Some days, it seems as though the water is calm, and that the Enemy is far away, and has even forgotten us. Then it is easy to forget what he can do, and our hope rises and rises, and the sky seems bright and clear, and we imagine our Tower reaching into the sky forever, full of hope and made of wonder and strength and caught breath, and on those days we are sure, and we forget the Enemy, and we pour ourselves into our work, and we build as though we have an endless stream of tomorrows before us.

Sometimes, there are those who just sit, staring down into the water, watching it rise, waiting for it to reach them, or for the Enemy to rise up and take them. (The water never reaches them; it is always the Enemy; he comes for everyone in the end, as far as I can see.)

But I keep building. I think: if I can get this ceiling finished, and those windows into the wall so I can have a good view out over the water, and finish the stairs, it will be very comfortable, and I will be able to start building the next level up, and I might even gain on the water, and put some distance between myself and it... I have heard of it being done, but I have never seen it. I do not really know.

The Tower reaches far down into the darkness, but we

feel that we know so much about it because of the stories that we tell each other — about its great victories and heartbreaking defeats, its trials and torments, its secret places and great halls, its passages and doorways through which beauty has paraded, and horror stalked, through which song and blood have flowed. So have I heard...

I have also heard it said, by a man named Aeschylus, that long ages ago, each one of us knew when the Enemy would come for us. But we all stood waist deep in the water then, and we built nothing, and knew nothing of a life above the water.

But then the knowledge of the time when the Enemy would come was taken from us, and in return, we were given hope — hope that the Enemy might forget us; hope that if we work and build hard enough, we might rise above the water, out of the Enemy's reach, away from the deathly chill of his grasp — and so today, there is always hope. We have traded knowledge for hope.

The Enemy came for a friend yesterday; he was one of the quiet ones, he went beneath the water quickly; it is almost as if the Enemy wants to be merciful about it sometimes.

But I do not really know; I have never seen it.

And now, there is building to do. Because everywhere, there is water.

Some of the more attractive incidents described in the following story — the stuffing of windows and doorways with the bodies of the dead, the scientists engaged in research while fighting rages around them, the officer attending to his wig — these all did happen during Napoleon's retreat from Moscow, according to contemporary accounts.

It is also certainly true that the entire complement of the First Division of the Young Guard (General Berthezene's command) were lost during the campaign in Russia. Of his six battalions (approx. 8,000 men), not a single soldier was left to answer in roll call.

Of the 50,000 that were the total of the Guard (the Young, Middle and Old combined), 1,100 survived.

As for Napoleon's death on the roof of a burning library outside Borodino — I'm absolutely sure that that happened.

BERTHEZENE

UNDER A TREE ON A HILL, from the top of which is visible everything that is about to concern us, gather two shades, both recently departed from the world.

One is, or was, French, and is, or was, a Soldier of the Line, his uniform torn and dirty in a manner that leaves us little doubt as to the unenviable nature of his demise.

His companion — but wait, the word is suggestive of a friendship, so let us say his *colleague* — is a different affair. He is clearly not a peasant, or any other sort of villein. His dress identifies him as a Russian, and an officer, and — forgive the allusion — a gentleman, and used to enjoying a greater degree of comfort and civility than the Frenchman; nevertheless — and here is the proof that some things cannot be postponed and will wait for no man — he is just as dead as the other, just as incorporeal, and just as much a matter of spirit.

Below these two, stretched out on a plain of gold and green under the fading warmth of the autumn sun (a minor detail, the temperature, now of interest to neither of the two watchers), an army, a hundred and more thousand strong, streams out of a burning city.

The French ghost speaks: "So, they leave Moscow."

"Yes. They resisted the notion, but there was never a doubt, after the fires."

"Look how many there are! And do they not still bear themselves as much like the host of some new heaven as they did when they arrived?"

"Hah! Oh, my Gallic friend, heaven indeed! If any of them still hold to *that* idea, it is most surely a delusion. They are fewer, by half at least, riven by disease and battle — though they are still many, and though their standards fly, and their officers yet ride horses; they are most certainly thinner, by rank and by substance. And it was only fifty days ago that you arrived here! And now, the winter comes for your countrymen..."

"Ah, winter! Let it take care of itself. See how warm the scene looks, how golden that sun. But is it deliberately, my Russian friend, that you distract us from the state of your Capital? Even your adversary, my own dear Emperor, whose star led us here, pales at its condition..."

"You have my measure there; I admit it, I grow sad at the sight. Look at what has become of her, my City, the population all fled, the palaces burning pyres, the avenues and streets desolate, left to the columns of smoke and flame that play quadrille between the houses. All empty, even now of the conqueror, who flees in the face of the fires set around him."

"He does, he leaves... with all his army, in such chaos and so badly drilled he departs, amazed that the Russian abandoned his capital so thoroughly, or at all! And no less amazed at the fires which roar behind him, denying him his prize..."

"The prize will mean nothing soon, my friend, whether it be held or lost. The agents of the Czar have denied the invader food and drink and shelter from the coming winter. In just days there will be cold such that your soft European hides cannot imagine. Your Spaniards, your French, your Prussians, your Italians, they may think they know what a brisk day is, and how to turn their collars up, but I swear, even as they expire, they will beg for death! And they have been warned so very well..."

47

"Indeed they have. And there has been no shortage of Russians to belabour the point, just as you do now. And so, how shall we write it?"

And one of the ghostly pair sits at a table of the finest Swedish hardwood, and takes up an exquisitely weighted silver pen, and readies the first of the sheets of vellum.

"Shall we mention, perhaps, that the flames that consume Moscow are the same as those which melted the wings of Icarus, son of Daedalus?"

"True perhaps, but too poetic for our audience and our purpose. I think we can take that as a given, just between us? Let us limit ourselves to the facts. Like this, perhaps..." and the shade of the Russian officer proceeds to inscribe:

> *"Ranked and ordered,*
> *bearing high their flags and eagles,*
> *four and eight abreast,*
> *weapons squared and horse held straight,*
> *first a thousand*
> *then ten thousand*
> *then a hundred thousand,*
> *forgetting*
> *that they leave the city hungry,*
> *forgetting*
> *because there are so many of them,*
> *and the noise and clamour and din are so great,*
> *and the spectacle distracts them,*
> *and everything seems to be endless.*
> *The Grande Armée fills the world!*
> *from one horizon to the other.*
> *The Emperor proclaims to all*
> *that his star is in the sky."*

"Large talk, my friend, but let us let it pass. But look on their baggage train, and what they have filled it to bursting with! All the gold, all the silver, all the books and tapestries, all the fine clothing and paintings... all shall come to nothing."

"I fear that you may have something there; but then, as always in war, we shall see..."

"So many dead or eloped already, and yet there are still so many left who do not think of what slopes so roughly toward them, just a few days hence. Look, see those fine carriages, carrying the foreign women, and their servants, their portmanteaux and hat boxes..."

"It is so warm, the sky so clear and blue..."

"So you said. Oh, the sky will stay clear for your companions, have no fear on that account; as clear as ice. Look, Saxons, Poles, Spaniards and Austrians... did you bring all of Europe with you?"

"They gathered most easily. It was not hard."

"Quite so. How unfortunate that the land they thought to take was already possessed. And now they depart, and the only Russian soil that they can lay claim to will serve them as a grave. How shall we put this? We must introduce Berthezene, you know..."

> *"And behind, left among the flames*
> *so outrageously and well set,*
> *with his eight thousand Young Guard,*
> *all but two of which are past their prime use,*
> *and shamble where they should*
> *most fearlessly and in order stand,*
> *Berthezene, one of the Corsican's favoured sons,*
> *is charged with the guarding*
> *of the Grand Collective Rump*

— as the one hundred and forty thousand,
and the fifty thousand horse of all description,
and the six hundred pieces,
with powder and shot for each,
and every bauble that the horde
could unscrew, tear up, decamp or lift
— Oh the weight, and breadth, and height,
and what a sight! —
is made to file out of the gate
and take the road — oh my,
even ghosts as we might blanch at this —
all the way back to Borodino."

"Fairly said, I have no issue. And now, look, at Napoleon's command they will destroy anything of value that has not already been burnt by the Czar's own saboteurs.

*

"General Berthezene, unable to trust his own troops to do the work of setting the charges, so dishevelled and easily distracted (by loot, among other things) are they, has pressed into service an army of prisoners, of local citizenry, of foreigners, the old, the sick, the wounded — and these are forced to dig and mine under the Kremlin and the palaces, and to place explosives

When that is done, and the *Grande Armée* has all but left the City, and there are ten thousand Cossacks under Winzingerode in the vicinity of the outer suburbs to the east and making their way towards the centre, Berthezene commands his troops to remove themselves, which they are happy to do on account of their booty and the fact that they are left alone in the city, and have been restraining themselves somewhat and, primarily, because they are regiments of the Young Guard.

Berthezene himself lights the fuses, and those fuses are so long that it is not until he and his men have almost rejoined the body of the the *Grande Armée* that the centre of the City and the Kremlin and the palaces and the storehouses of the rich and noble are blown to pieces in sudden fire and unbearable noise, along with the thin crowd of the common and base who have run in, on seeing Berthezene and his men depart, thinking to help themselves to what is left of the possessions of their Russian masters, or just to wander loudly and disdainfully through the hallways and dance in the boudoirs, or to lie on a Lady's bed, or to lord it over a Count's chamber pot, or to clear the kitchens or the workshops of what can be taken — no matter their motivation, they are all disintegrated, each and every one, so that in the hail of glass and masonry and well-turned wooden shards that rains upon the city, there is a garnish of blood and torn limbs and riven pieces of flesh and bone, and clothing, and shoes, all stripped and torn and bloody... in this way the destruction of what was left of the better part of Moscow was brought about."

"That was a longish passage, my friend. Let us call it apocryphal, and leave it at that."

"With that I cannot argue. But I felt the need to establish, for posterity, the true provenance of this singular train of events."

"You are no doubt right; we can never be too careful with the causes of all this, and that train of events that you mention. They will try to forget the typhus, you know. But now, let us attend. Advance, the tale of General Berthezene!"

And soon, upon the vellum these words appear:

When the Grande Armée crossed the Neimen,
full of the flush of adolescence,
its armour and will impenetrable,
the Emperor's host, gathered from every quarter,
six hundred thousand by some accounts,
and if that is an overstating of the case,
it is not by much.
And in the Young Guard's First Division,
General Berthezene's was the sole brigade,
and his brigade was six battalions,
and the long shadow
that those eight thousand cast
was a reputation fit for legend!

When they passed, the regiments of the line would
make way, and present arms in silence.
An officer of the line would salute
A sergeant of the Guard, and
the enemy would pray that they would never,
this day or any other, face the Guard —
the Young, or Middle, or Old —
for upon each Division
the mantle of hardened steel
wrought by the Empire's will
rests equally, and with awful precision.

*

How General Berthezene's heart had swelled with pride, not too many weeks ago; to see his regiments, his *voltigeurs* and *tirailleurs*, his batteries, his supply trains, his standards and eagles, all flourishing under his watch, and the eyes of his men would turn in admiration as he rode by, and when word had gone out that the Emperor himself had made mention of General Berthezene as an exemplar of generalship, his men had cheered, and every one of them was glad to be among the First Division of the Young Guard.

And the Young Guard had entered Moscow in better order than most, because even though disease and privation had cut down so many, and the *Armée* was half what it had been, still the Guard had been held back at Borodino when the battle there had finally been joined, and the army of the dead had recruited none of Berthezene's men for its ranks.

*

Moscow is just a few days behind them, and the cold is come, suddenly, as if from nowhere. Of the eight thousand that began, Berthezene now has just five thousand left in any sort of order; and most of these no longer have soldiering on their mind, so much as a simple regretting of their current situation.

The trees that tower darkly above them, stripped to their tops to become corpses themselves, offer those who trudge below them no shelter or word of solace. Each man nurses his own secret horror at his weakness amidst this immensity, and at the vast distance between him and his home. It is a gradual destitution in which the depression of the soul keeps company with the debilitation of the body. It is destitution of which the end is certain.

They march on, any hope of order lost, the line strung out and disintegrating into groups of soldiers and stragglers, threading through horses and men dead or dying from exhaustion or wounds or the cold which has now come upon them with a vengeance beyond knowing.

Berthezene's pride is a thing of the past. His men are

falling around him like rain. They collapse into the snow and are left to fend for themselves, which is to say that the Cossacks and the peasants will find them if the cold does not, and that will be the end of them, at the leisure of their enemy, which will not be hurried.

*

General Berthezene, the sergeant is rasping, and he rouses me from something I would like to have called sleep, but it is not, the cold will not allow such things. We are too exhausted to sleep. *The officers*, the sergeant is saying. *They are not there...*

Not there? I say, and before I can ask their whereabouts, he says that they are all dead, and that the few among the enlisted men who will answer to an order are answering to him, a sergeant. *Then carry on, and take a horse*, I tell him, and keep them together as well as you can.

My own horse will soon die under me, or I under it. It reels in the cold, and has almost no strength left.

I have taken a greatcoat from a private in the infantry. His corpse had no further use for it. Where he got the coat, I do not know, but it is issue, from one of our allies in Europe, I can see that, and at least it is a winter coat. They gave *us* summer uniforms! My hands and feet have not frozen solid. That pleases me.

*

We have reached Borodino, the site of our engagement just weeks ago with 120,000 Russians under Kutusov; the battle that the Emperor finally achieved and the adversary finally allowed. 30,000 corpses lie half-devoured, rotting in the snow, circlets of skeletons guarding hills and redoubts gaze down upon us. None of us say much, my men and I. There are so many dead here that it feels impossible to notice even one. There are so many ghosts to haunt us, and we were here so recently, and, worse, it is our doing.

We keep our eyes down, and I hear my men whispering, it *is the site of the great battle*, and we do not look at the trees all broken down to the ground line, at the smashed artillery and wagons that litter the ridges and roads, at the endless sea of broken and dismembered bodies.

We pass the battlefield, and all the while, we die a little more with every step. There is no *Grande Armée* any more.

*

The town of Borodino is empty. Some vagary of this vast traffic of humanity and materiel has left it silent and desolate while I lead (*if you can call it leading…*) my men through the streets. The buildings are hollowed by fire, and there are bodies perched and hanging from every piece of wood or masonry that protrudes or offers even the meanest purchase for a piece of flesh or bone. Borodino most surely is a town of the dead.

A man and a woman have died before me in the gathering darkness. Frozen solid as they leaned against a tree, standing as if they wait for something.

Everywhere is destruction. No one speaks now. The night has fallen, the ice has taken on the darkness that presses us so hard from every quarter, and offers no respite but death. I hear the sounds of movement around me, and there are moans and sighs, and there are forms which I suppose to be men or women, but I cannot be sure and I do not care. No one calls for their general.

My horse is dead. I slit his poor throat, then warmed my hands in the wound.

In silence we depart the center of Borodino, like travelers through a gate of hell. I have no idea how many men from my regiments remain. I know it is not many. No one reports to me. I do not ask.

*

On the outskirts of Borodino, a crowd has gathered. We see them, their backs to us, there is something there that makes us quicken our faltering, freezing steps, and we join the throng. And then we see a building. According to the words above its doors, it is the town's library.

The mass around the building numbers in the hundreds. They, and soon we as well, are mesmerized by the warmth that radiates from its stone walls.

*

And near the wreck of Borodino
where no breath is drawn
and no soul moves but
that bland spirit that in keeping with its nature
riles for retribution,
and shudders towards the centre,
its frozen claw outstretched,

he in whom resides the Empire
has taken to the shelter
of the only building
neglected by artillery and fire
and so left to stand intact.

He paces on the rooftop,
seeing glass in hand
and scours the heavens for his star —

but it does not appear,
and flames burn hot below
and the flesh that boils and turns
is far from caring any more.

Barely human, sense recoils.

*

"How sorry is this sight?"
    "He could not hold forever. The centre never can."

*

I can see him! Through the crowd of frozen, wounded, and all-but-dead — he is up there, on the roof. The Emperor, himself! — he paces about, stopping every few steps to curse and look up at the night sky through his telescope. He sweeps his gaze across the firmament, stopping here and there, looking for his star, but never finding it. Although it is a clear and cloudless night, there is not a single star to be seen; and the sky is a dark featureless plain, relieved only by the pale disc of the moon that has appeared above the horizon, from where it is rising slowly above the scene, illuminating all equally with a minacious light.

Between the breathing grenadier and the rigor-mortised cavalry colonel who has been dead in his saddle for a day and a half; between the smashed and overturned artillery piece and the wagon that once held hay sitting somehow unscathed and untouched behind the shelled-out church; between the mother holding the body of her baby and the field marshal who ordered that a thousand Russian prisoners be put to the sword — between all these and each other, and between all these and my own breath which freezes almost before it exits me, I can longer discern any difference.

The Emperor curses and hurls his glass away. He snatches another from one of his aides, and raises it desperately to the sky, muttering as he begins his search again. As I watch, his officers move away, glances exchanged. Even faithful Berthier leaves, and soon Bonaparte is left alone.

A murmuring arises in the crowd.

The windows of the library are closed, and through the shutters is visible the flickering of a light that can only mean fire. The crowd surges forward, for there must be heat! And only when they begin tearing at the doors and windows, trying to gain access to the interior of the building, do I see that the entrances are barred not with doors or sheets of wood, but are stacked full with bodies, laid like cordwood so as to keep the extremes of wind and temperature at bay.

The dead in their hundreds are piled up in the window bays, doing a final service in the place of destroyed glass; and in doorways lie the frozen bodies of infantry, and cavalrymen, and generals and wives and peasants, all substitutes for doors long taken and burned for heat.

The people begin to pound and tear at the bodies, ripping them from their resting places, and hurling them, in the case of the few who possess the strength, and dragging them tortuously, in the case of most — aside, so that dead bodies soon form grisly passes into the flame-lit interior of the building.

And the crowd pours into the library, and I am swept along with them — not against my will, because I have no will any more, and because just the promise of heat is breath-taking — and then I am in a hall lined with books, and the officers that have deserted the Corsican and come down from the roof are rushing past me, fear and loathing on their faces, and I see that fires have been set under the tables, consuming them, and that the flames are being fed by books, pulled from the shelves, and torn apart, and thrown onto the pyres, and there are bodies among the flames as well.

The reprieve from the cold is too much, too instant and overwhelming. Now I am burning. I realize with horror that the smell of charred flesh makes me think of food and my own hunger before any thought of revulsion attains the place it should. The smoke thickens and the tumult is soon intolerable as the rooms and hallways become crowded with shuffling, frostbitten invalids, carrying armfuls of books with which they appear to be intent on fuelling fires over which to cook themselves or someone else.

I am in hell.

*

I do not know how long it takes me, but I force a passage to the outside. Smoke streams from the doorways and windows, and flames have begun to leap from the upper storey windows. The air is full of burning fragments of books and manuscripts, fluttering and swooping through the air like fireflies escaping into the night.

A Russian shell lands nearby, directly in a group who are slicing flesh from bodies and placing the pieces in a cooking pot placed over a fire of books. The blast eviscerates them all instantly. Blood and scalding soup, of whom or what I have no idea, covers me.

And now I am beside myself, incapable of thought or navigation, weary beyond humanity or pain. I find myself at the foot of the library wall, collapsed or collapsing, I cannot tell which. As I wipe the blood from my eyes with one hand, my other hand is resting on a bundle on the ground beside me. It moves against my touch.

When I regain my senses a few — or many, I have no idea — minutes later — or an hour, or several hours — the coat that I had been wearing has been removed and lies near me, torn and bloody beyond any reasonable notion of use. It has been replaced, through being placed around my shoulders, by a heavy fur coat, of the type the local peasants use. It is roughly made, but suited to its purpose.

A child, a young boy perhaps ten years old, stands before me, regarding me and saying nothing.

*

"He can barely stand it, poor Berthezene. Perhaps he is a more sensitive soul than either he or we realized..."

"He is a general for the Corsican! He should have plenty of tolerance for evisceration and blood and shit, of any hue."

"Well, a reed can bend, and bend, but sooner or later it will break... and they are all so far from home."

"My friend, forget this Berthezene, he is of no importance..."

> *The Emperor seeks his rising star*
> *In an empty sky from a burning deck*
> *And in clawing, heaving, hoar and ice*
> *Fire consumes the narrow house.*
> *Heaven is not there*
> *to swallow the smoke*

*

Borodino is behind us.

We are struggling through an endless wilderness of snow and ice. We are dying.

The Russians persecute us relentlessly. Their Cossacks, their infantry, their peasants, all kill us whenever they can.

We have no formations, we fall apart, each one a tattered coat on a cage of bone and withering flesh.

The column of smoke from Borodino haunts us like the Emperor's missing star.

I did not think it could get colder.

It is colder.

A circle of men and women around a fire died where they sat, roasted on one side and frozen solid on the other. Do not sit near a fire in this; the heat will kill you. Men eat corpses to survive. The urine of horses, if drunk straight from the horse, is hot.

If we see someone about to end their own misery, no one moves to stop him. We envy him.

*

> *The River Berezina comes upon them like a wall,*
> *there is no egress from this*
> *save a pair of broken bridges,*
> *or through eighty thousand Russians,*
> *all fed and warmed and honed*
> *like a sharpened butcher's blade,*
> *replete with such untempered propensities*
> *for revenge and nemesis,*
> *and each Russian will take*
> *as many Frenchmen down to hell*
> *as hell will take.*

*

The river Berezina has stopped them. They gather in a disordered mass on its banks as dawn breaks. Ice flakes sweep through them, driven by the approaching storm, cutting into the flesh of man and horse alike. In the gathering light, they can see the Russian columns approaching.

The child has stayed with him. There has been no asking, no questions or stories. Just the constant presence, the watching face. It was the child who put the coat on him, the child who found some charred horse flesh on which he restored his strength, and the child who stayed with him on the march from Borodino, and who now stands beside him, hand gathered in his, in front of the ice and waters of the Berezina.

*

And so now the shades' work is almost done.

"Eighty thousand! And every single one of them desperate to cross this one little Russian river... all across these two little Russian bridges..."

"You make light..."

"And the bridges are broken."

"Then they will be repaired, and see? Look now. Let the children of France marvel forever at the bravery of the sappers who work until they die in the freezing waters, suffocated by the cold, crushed by the ice, swept away by the current, one after the other, until the bridges are repaired."

"It is good and selfless work, it is true, any man will admit that, and must further admit to awe."

"And while the Russian armies circle round and gain position, these titans struggle through the day and then through the night by the light of the enemy campfires, while the weather proves itself to be more Russian than a Russian, so ideally do the temperature and wind and sleet all conspire to keep the river from freezing, and it flows rough and hard, and all the while panic grows, and grows..."

"This can be written easily, I think."

Chaos, dark, and manic,
Though the day is bright and clear,
Eighty thousand, heaving, gasping fear,
Hell's midsummer is about to solstice early,
And about to solstice here...

*

Berthezene sees a group below a tree. It is the remnants of
the Academy of Sciences, occupied with the geometry of
snow flakes, and the seeking of an academically reputable
explanation for the direction of the wind which tears at the
waters before them. Beside them, a Count who has lost his
regiments sits on a snow-covered tree stump, powdering
his wig.

And as the night proceeds, the Russian artillery, relocating
so that it might better slaughter, finally reaches its redoubt,
and taking aim, proceeds to sow terror wide. The Count loses
his wig, with his head still in it.

Masses moan, and heave, and clamour, the weak fall below
the hooves and wheels of their own countrymen, to the side,
or into the water and are swept away. The Russian shells reap
a rich harvest, such that no fragment of them ever touches
the ground, the flesh that they gorge on is so tightly packed.

Among the *Armée*, new leaders rise and fall, dynasties are
deposed in a breath by a Russian shell or the blind weight of
a stampeding horse.

*

My sergeant comes up to me. He takes me by the arm and
cries, his tears turn to hoarfrost on his cheeks. *They are gone,*
he says, *who,* I say. *The men, the regiments, the entire division,*
he says, *all that are left are you, General, and I, and half a gun*

63

crew, who have lost their gun. *We together are all that remains of our eight thousand.*

This is my command, then. Half a crew without a gun, this old sergeant, and a boy. We are the First Division of the Young Guard, all of it. There is no more.

As a fog settles around us with the dying of the wind, the miasma that has clutched my own mind clears. The boy says his first words to me. *The horsemen,* and he looks beyond us, and I turn, and I see them coming.

The enemy's artillery has gone quiet with the coming of the dawn, and the Russian General Wittgenstein's cavalry, another part of his 50,000, is sweeping down towards us, sabres bared, throats roaring, and before them scatters, crying for God, our sorry horde, broken and disarrayed to a new pitch again.

The mass of us surges with renewed and thoughtless determination to the bridges. Officers force a path through the press, crushing all in their way beneath the hooves of their horses and the wheels of their carriages. A group of Spanish horse cut their own way across the bridge closest to us, pushing unfortunates into the swollen river. As many drown or fall to the side as make it across, and as the movement of the crowd takes us across the bridge, the boy and I cling close to each other. I turn to my old sergeant, to see him fall away into the torrent, his chest blooming a red rose sprouted from the impact of a musket ball.

Two carriages of nobility and whores careen and collide, and under their weight the bridge sags precipitously, and from their cases and bags and chests spills their hoard of gold and silver coins, and icons of Jesus and Madonnas, and reliquaries and precious books and crystal chandeliers, and with a clear mind and eye, I see the boy slip from my grasp into the water.

I watch as if from a distance as I reach for him, falling with the looted objects and the carriages and the screaming horses into the water, which swallows them all with equal ease and finality, folding over them like a winding sheet.

The boy is lying still, unmoving in the current where he has fallen beneath a frozen sheet of water. I take up a fallen soldier's musket, and strike desperately with the weapon, until I have made a hole through which I can reach into the depths below.

And I reach for him, but now the boy has been carried along by the current, and as I am lying down, stretched out on the ice, my arm submersed to the shoulder and numb in the freezing water, and my heart beginning to weep and break for the young boy, who is so young, and who knows nothing of bayonets and cavalry charges and flechettes and firing squads and typhus and gangrene and everything else that we have brought with us, and which we have visited on them and which they have visited on us — I see, in the shifting of light and shadow in the water, and the shapes of drowned men and horses, and carriages turned into watery tombs, a movement that comes towards us, and there is a figure, a woman, I am sure, and I see her clearly as she rises from the black depths towards us, and she takes the boy with one hand, and she takes my wrist in a cold grip with the other, and she brings us together, so that I take hold of the boy, and with all my strength I pull him towards me and up, and through the hole, and onto the surface of the ice, and instantly he is laid down I turn back, and the woman is no longer there, and the water is empty.

*

The shade of the Russian speaks. "Has your general not come a long way..."

"Further than his men. But here he stays."

"Your Corsican brought with him enough grist and gristle to feed this maw for a long time yet."

"And there are tens of thousands of morsels still to be served up. The hunger for lives is insatiable. And see! Where the flesh leads, the gold and chattels follow soon enough."

"No hunger will be sated with Berthezene, or the boy, that much I suspect. The details are unknowable, true, but their destinies are certain."

"I will wager that he dies."

*

The eviscerated corpse of the *Armée* crawls, finally, bloody, across the bridge.

The carnage here is complete.

Berthezene lies on the snow of the river bank, dying.

*

Everything is so large. I do not have long.

I am so cold, to my core. The child kneels with me. He leans close and whispers thanks for the episode just played out on the ice. And he adds: *I shall have no leaders, for look what leaders have done.*

I am thinking clearly still, the clarity of ice and death and peace all together, and in that, I can see that my own is upon me. I raise my hand to touch the child's face, and see a band around my wrist, where the woman's grasp has burned into my skin. At the sight, I feel my breathing ease, and the last thing in me that was resisting gives up the fight.

I hear the sound of horses approaching, at their leisure.

Go, I tell the child, and he rises and retreats to the bridge.

I cannot turn my head now. I lie prone on the ice, with my breathing more shallow with each pass, and I feel the ice forming over my eyes and in my mouth.

I can see the boy depart the bridge to the other side of the river and I watch, as if it is played out on a dimming stage, as he is approached by a colonel on a horse, but he sends the man away. And a scientist from the Institute approaches him, but the boy sends him away. And then a priest, fresh from blessing corpses, approaches him, but he sends the man of god away as well.

Hooves arrive in my field of vision, the iron-shod monsters of a Russian warhorse. I can see, as my failing, occluded eyes scale its heights, a Russian officer lean into his pommel, taking in my condition, and beside him, another cavalryman.

A general, here he is, he says, but of course I do not understand his speech.

Yes, here he is. We had so many, says his companion in French, and so of course I can understand that, and they turn their horses away.

Но все-таки, я не понимаю ....

Ni moi...

THE ONE A DOG RUNS TO

CEBA HAS BEEN TAKEN.

I shall describe how and by whom presently, but first, you should understand that there is one male for whom her skin is the dark musk honey scent of all women; for whom her eyes are the eyes of every goddess, every female bodhisattva, dakini, temple whore, all these things at once; her touch is the sum of everything, all become one, the universe into one experience, all from the recollection of a touch, of skin barely brushed against skin.

It has been this way since they were young; and she, Ceba, knows this, and secretly she feels the same for him, and there was a time that they swore, each to themselves but not to each other, because of mountains of shyness and fear, and on account of neither of them daring to test the shy, tentative creature that their love was — that they would, if they could, grow old together, and that they would, in a world filled to overflowing with so much uncertainty and sorrow, be together, if they could; if only the world would let them.

Now, the taking of Ceba went like this: she and her sister were carrying firewood to the monastery when they encountered a tulku on his way back from inspecting farms at the end of the valley. Naturally, they fell to their knees on the hard white rocks and prostrated themselves. They meant not to raise their eyes, of course — but just as the tulku was passing them, his horse, or Ceba and her sister, or all three, disturbed a Hot Spring snake, which had no business being there, so far from its normal environs, and the serpent, in its hissing and rearing and then its serpentine slithering away quickly, and the two women, in their fright at seeing the creature so close to them, and in fact at never having seen one before, leaping upwards from their prostrated position and shrieking in animal fright and surprise — all these things together caused the lama's horse to rear, and so tip its rider onto the very hard and white rocks from which the snake had emerged.

The snake had instantly disappeared, to become the stuff of local legend; the horse had bolted, wanting no part in the proceedings, legendary or otherwise; and Ceba and her sister, once the maelstrom of dismounting and yelling attendants and whirling robes and panic and accusations and the twitching, speechless bleeding of the tulku's life onto the rocks as a blossoming of wet, dark red were all resolved, at least enough for order to be regained — the two women were tied and trussed, their arms behind their backs, and they were dragged, their boots removed and their feet bleeding, behind the horses the rest of the way back to the monastery.

The women made the journey in a silence of terror, their breathing ragged with stumbling, and heaving with the exertion of keeping up with the horses.

The tulku, cooling in the descending evening and slung across his recovered horse, had entered the void he had so long contemplated.

*

The Master's master has sent a letter. It is brought by a monk from Gyumey monastery, four days away. The monk in question spent those four days cursing his karma; spent it complaining to himself that the time of year could not be worse; grumbling that he should be sent to this place, when he was feeling so unwell... he arrives late, wheezing, his breath cutting into him like a knife, coughing bloody lace into the night air as he climbs the path up to the monastery. He seems too young for the disease, even here, but there you go... the letter he hands to the Master says this:

We are about to hold puja to celebrate the Dalai Lama's birthday. As part of the celebrations, special food will be thrown to the animals. You are to supply wet intestines, two skulls, blood, and two full human skins, all of which must be promptly delivered.

On reading the letter and sending the monk on his way bearing reassurance that the materials will be supplied on time (the monk will make it back to Gyumey, but the damage will be done, and he will be dead within a month), the Master summons the young monk Tenzin to his gompa.

Gompa is a charitable use of the name; it might be best to forget what you expect a gompa to be; this one is nothing grand, it is a jumble of small and lightless rooms, either carved into the rock or constructed from the hewn fragments of it (so you see there are two ways of making a room) and there are a few rough stupas there as well, in which it is generally accepted that there are relics of various kinds — a thumb here, a thighbone there, pieces of a nameless skull and jawbone in the one near the dried up spring... all this religion sits heavily on the summit of an old volcanic eruption of a ridge, where it is hidden from the sight of the town by more of the same order of convolutions.

Gompas aside, this town has something which the other towns in the area do not. A monastery sits on its edge, elevated above it by a few feet of rock. At its centre is a hall which is light in the mornings and dark in the afternoons, and lined with dry corpses, each enthroned on a platform covered with old and brittle golden brocade and the dust of crumbling robes and dried flesh. They are the prior abbots of the monastery, and now here is why, and how, they come to be here.

Near the Master's gompa there is a cell, carved into the rock. It is very old, and it is where the previous abbots have all ended their lives, walled in and brought food by their monks, which they retrieve with wasting hands, reaching out of the darkness through small crevices. When they die, their bodies already preserved by their diet of leaves and barks, the cave is opened, and their mummifying remains are retrieved and installed in the hall of the Masters. There are 33 desiccated Masters there now, and when this Master dies, there will be 34.

*

It is to Master's gompa, then, that the monk Tenzin is headed.

Tenzin has been a good pupil. Not only did he complete the Chenrezig initiation in his early years, but he also did not have to repeat any part of the instruction; he was never punished or scourged for failing even a single one of the examinations; he was never beaten for forgetting verses in recital; and he has even, to his credit, been chosen to assist Master in the rites with the novices. Tenzin has been an excellent student, and there is talk of his future.

Tenzin knows nothing of the letter from Gyumey as he climbs the path to the gompa. When one of the novices came with word that Master had summoned him, he had been in meditation, and he continues his practice as he ascends the twisting path, turning the wheel of dharma as he goes, walking slowly, mindfully, taking his time over the *samdhinirmocana sutra.*

He labours only half-heartedly against the unskillful burden of pride, pride held on account of knowing it so well, and because he has bettered so many of the senior monks in debate on its verses, and because he knows that he, Tenzin, is unraveling the Buddha's mind... The thought of Ceba arises in his mind, gossamerred in a mist that is a combination of memory, anticipation and desire. Mindfully, he places it aside. Aside, but within reach.

As Master's gompa comes into view, crowning the ragged ridge ahead of him, Tenzin is contemplating the thousand-armed form of Chenrezig.

> *Due to this merit may I soon*
> *attain the enlightened state of Chenrezig*
> *that I may be able to liberate*
> *all sentient beings from their sufferings.*
>
> *May the precious bodhi mind*
> *not yet born arise and grow.*
> *May that born have no decline,*
> *but increase forever more.*
>
> *Due to the positive potential accumulated*
> *by myself and others in the past, present*
> *and future, may anyone who merely sees,*
> *hears, remembers, touches or talks to me*
> *be freed in that very instant from all sufferings*
> *and abide in happiness forever.*

Master is the incarnation of Chenrezig. Master is Chenrezig, and Chenrezig is Master; there is no difference. Chenrezig sees everything. The bodhisattva's eyes, one in each of his thousand hands, never look away from the world, never close or look away; and so like all masters, Master sees everything. Tenzin, too, aspires to clear away the dust of delusion, so that he too may see everything... and there will be no difference between Tenzin, and Master, and Chenrezig...

Tenzin is decided on this: he will, one day, be Master of the monastery, and he will follow this current Master, this sick and dying old man who sees everything, into the cave, and then he will follow him mummified into the hall, and there he and Master will sit with the other 33 masters until the coming of Maitreya, and they will all sit there together, for the sake and enlightenment of all sentient beings...

*

Master's room is dark. It always is. Tenzin imagines for a moment how total it will be, the blackness, when Master enters the cave. The shadows in Master's room today are as heavy as the mountains outside.

Master is sitting reading by the light of a small fire. Another monk stands near him, waiting in silence. Master looks up, sees Tenzin in the doorway, and looks at a spot on the floor. Tenzin takes his place and says nothing.

The other monk is Gephel. He has brainless, expressionless eyes, and that sloping brow which is well known to reduce the brain-bearing capacity of the skull. Gephel has the thin lips that idiots have, and across his cheeks and shaved head are the scars of his life outside the monastery. He is no match for anyone in the debates, and for that Gephel is the object of jokes and derision. This causes him no distress, though, for no one would dare say anything to his face; if they did, he would beat them senseless, or if such disrespect came from a peasant, to death, and that has happened. Gephel has no interest in the sutras, but makes up for this with unquestioning, blind obedience. The end result of Gephel is that he is respected, feared, appreciated and ridiculed, all at once.

The Master leans forward and drops the paper onto the fire. "Lash them both," he says to Gephel, as the flames flare then settle down again, becoming a soft drone of light again in the space of a breath. "One hundred times, then tie them to the rocks at Drolma Pass. Leave them to Chenrezig and their karma. If they survive the night, lash them again."

Gephel looks up. "The children?"

The Master says nothing, and waves at the door without looking at it. Gephel bows carelessly and leaves. The karma of the runaway serf and his family is about to bloom.

The Master reaches for the letter from Gyumey. His hand is shaking with the infirmity that has been gathering around him; he grows weaker every day, his bones strain against his skin, his eyes have collapsed into their sockets. They focus on less and less, retreating into the darkness inside him.

"We need material, for rites," the Master says. "Two individuals."

Tenzin wonders at being given the task. He does not shy from his duty; he has assisted with blinding and removing hands and hamstrings, and has administered the lash himself, although only once and not expertly. That did not go well; death came too quickly, while the lash was still being applied; such things should not be rushed, but he was inexperienced. Now, he knows which arteries to stay away from, and how deep to go.

If there is a true practitioner in these matters, it is Gephel. Gephel makes them suffer, and the pain must be felt, otherwise there is no point. Without the experience of pain, the skulls and intestines and skins are not as potent; they don't hold the power. Tenzin understands these things academically, but Gephel understands without thinking; in this matter, in Gephel, the formless ground seems to be unobscured. The ceremonial materials he provides are widely sought, such is his ability with pain. Gephel is much valued.

Tenzin recalls watching Gephel at work a few weeks ago, and the screams and pleas of the murderer under the knife and the hooks and the hot irons, and how quickly they degenerated into something beyond words. Even as they are torn, and bleed their lives screaming onto the earth, they grasp at life, seeking security in their egos. The hardship they endure is for the sake of others. All dharmas are empty. There is no suffering. The thousand eyes of Chenrezig miss nothing.

No one escapes their karma.

"Who?" Tenzin asks, nodding, feeling confident as he imagines the thousand eyes of Chenrezig turn onto him.

"Prisoners will do," says the Master. "Skull. Intestines. Blood, skin ... the Dalai Lama's birthday," he adds as an afterthought, letting the paper fall from his hand in Tenzin's direction. "Gephel can go with you, when he's finished up at the Pass."

Tenzin will meditate beforehand. Most of the other monks would not, and Gephel certainly will not; but Tenzin understands what is at stake, and will attend to the void before he sends anyone there. This procedure is rich in tantra, and must be attended to skillfully, for the sake of all sentient beings.

Thus all beings may attain bodhisattvahood.

Tenzin meditates on Chenrezig, the great, compassionate Avalokatesvara, Sahasrabhujalokeshvara, the bodhisattva with one thousand eyes, one in the palm of each of its one thousand hands, Chenrezig, Sahasrabhujalokeshvara who sees everything, the all-compassionate...

*

The street is not crowded. There is no market day, no religious procession or ceremony due. There is no music, no drums or horns; just the shuffling of feet and worn, faded fabric stirring in the dust of the late afternoon like brown leaves.

A group of novices are loitering, sunning themselves and talking loud, unskillful nonsense about the Lineage Tree when Tenzin arrives at the prison.

Gephel is not here yet. Tenzin sits against the wall of the prison a little way from the novices, amusing himself with their inanity and enjoying what heat there is left in the day.

Not far from where he sits, the prison is a few rooms in the basement of the monastery connected to a small roofless yard surrounded by a wall. Its entrance is a doorway made of blocks of stone that are crumbling and split with age; above the door the prison is named — too grandly, it seems to Tenzin — after the Snow Prison, the labyrinth below the Potala, in Lhasa.

The novices have moved on and the sun is almost behind the mountains by the time Gephel arrives. He has brought Jampa, the mastiff. Jampa, large, heavy with muscle and power, and the congealed blood of Drolma Pass drying on his face. The dog is familiar with the ramble of tunnels and chambers near the monastery. It pulls at the leash when it sees the entrance, pawing at the ground, whining.

Gephel wears a smile that is dark and empty, with no centre. The peasant and his wife must have gone well. Gephel stops between Tenzin and the prison door and looks, smiling, conspiratorial, down at the dog. They both seem to Tenzin to be happy, slightly touched with the delirium of the same anticipation.

Tenzin knows this game; Gephel likes to let the dog choose them. He will take the dog through the cells and through the prison yard, letting it rummage and sniff and growl, until it finds one which, for some dog-reason, it will choose.

Inside the door, Jetze, the prison mastiff, growls at being distracted from the severed hand he is chewing on. The two dogs give a perfunctory low growl, but are comfortable enough, in a wary, brotherly, sort of way. Tenzin extends his own hand to the dog. It sniffs at the offered appendage and then, disinterested by the familiarity, turns back to its meal.

Against the stench of dead blood and offal and shit that looms around them, and the constant buzzing of clouds of black flies, the light from outside refuses to offer any contest as they enter the prison.

*

The peasant will not look up at first. Tenzin doesn't know this one that Jampa ran to in the prison yard, heaving against the leash... and so karma unfolds, but of course, a dog does not understand karma, and Tenzin. He has studied the sutras. He doesn't know why the man was here in the prison. He was here; that is enough. The rest belongs to karma.

The room is dark and rank; grease lamps sputter,

possessed by the souls of burning dakinis. The kartika, the flaying knife, weighs in Tenzin's hand, glints of lamplight move along its curved blade. It is heavy, he feels it pulling down, towards the earth.

The rest belongs to karma.

*

The peasant is trying to say something. Through the blood and the fear, it is impossible to understand; or perhaps there are no words, perhaps it is the beast-without-language speaking now, from that place where they all seem to go towards the end. The peasant's eyes search Tenzin's, imploring, seeking some kind of blank animal sympathy, some dumb, elemental connection.

Tenzin visualises the hands of Chenrezig embracing the scene, holding everything in it with a type of clear, disconnected wonder, the eyes in the thousand palms dissolving karma in the blood and tears shed here. Everything is born and reborn continually, reborn as Tara, she who is the exquisite, the essence of compassion, from the tears of Chenrezig...

It is fortunate that Tenzin understands this. If he did not, there would be no one here to pause before the spectacle of the peasant's terror, in appreciation, in understanding of its true nature and value.

Endless wandering through the rounds of existence is caused by our grasping at egos as though they are real. This ignorant attitude is the demon of selfish concern for our welfare: we seek security for our egos; we want only pleasure and shun pain. But now this peasant must banish all selfish compulsion and endure hardship for the sake of all beings.

He makes a careful incision and begins removing the skin.

There is no more noise from the peasant; they usually make plenty, on account of which sometimes the tongue is removed early on, but then the donor will sometimes choke on the blood, and that is not ideal. This one lies there, quivering, looking, until Gephel puts out his eyes with the hot hooks, and then the only sound is that of the blade slicing, and the tearing of flesh as Tenzin cuts and Gephel uses the hook to pull at veins and tendons. At some point (and Tenzin is straight away ashamed that he was distracted, and not present in his work, and so did not notice) the peasant quietly dies.

Tenzin is disappointed. Gephel, who is opening the torso to remove the organs, has not noticed. It was too soon, but there is no need to say anything.

Jampa sits at Gephel's feet, watching attentively, rapt anticipation obvious on the dog's broad, handsome face.

Soon what needs to be in jars is in jars and ready to be transported to Gyumey. The skin has been scraped and washed clean, and is hanging, still steaming from the heat of the water, vaguely the shape of a man. The skin won't be allowed to dry. The vat of water steeped with herbs that will receive it sits on the floor, waiting.

What needs to be boiled so the flesh can be removed — the skull that will be inverted and decorated with beaten silver and used to hold blood and other fluids, and the bones that are going to be handled and gestured and pointed with, weaving into existence the various worlds — these lie submerged already, being stripped clean under a blanket of boiling fat and lye in the kettle.

"That was too quick." Gephel is wiping his hands on his heavy apron. He did notice, after all. He casts Tenzin a look, the look of a patient craftsman reminding an apprentice that he has much to learn. "We will take longer on the next one. Jampa, come. You can choose again."

Gephel and the dog leave. Tenzin is left alone in the room, standing before the table, the stone surface shining wet and red with blood, with nothing to do but wait.

Good; a moment of peace. Tenzin relishes it. A moment of emptiness, of the ground; the bodies of the dhyani buddhas, all manifest in Vairocana, *Nampar nangdze* ... a vision of serene and composed sky-born lotuses and deities, reposing in a field of infinite blue. He transcends the sweet metallic odour of blood which fills the room, the musky dark tang of rent bowels. The darkness of the room dissolves into the pure wisdom and light of tantra.

*

Just as the mountains of the Pure Land are forming among the clouds, he is brought back to the room by the sound of footsteps approaching. There is the shuffle of Gephel's sandals, his uncaring illiteracy resonating in every sliding, arrogant shuffle and slap; there is the impatient clatter of the dog's four sharp-nailed feet; and there is the uncomprehending, incoherent stagger of the prisoner that the dog had run to. That third set of steps gives nothing away; the sound is exhausted, confused and disoriented. It is too impersonal, too primal, for personality to have survived.

Tenzin dismisses the last of the mountains of the Pure Land and turns as Gephel and his entourage enter the room. Between the monk and his dog stands Ceba, bloody, her gaze sunken and fixed on the floor.

"Here", says Gephel, and he pushes her forward.

Tenzin says nothing. He is silent, but his heart is pounding. He forgets to breathe.

Gephel goes to the stone trough just inside the door. Meticulously, he begins washing his hands. "We shall take our time. The ritual implements will be strong."

Ceba sways on her bloodied feet. So that he does not have to look at her, Tenzin turns his head to the doorway, towards Gephel. Only when she is gone from his sight does he breathe. Gephel has straightened, facing Tenzin. In the half-light, he has become a gaunt, spectral figure, a ghost covered with gore and blood, hands wet with blood and water, head tilted like a wrathful deity on a thanka, emerging from the darkness as he steps towards Tenzin, who has still said nothing.

"Tenzin, are you ready?"

At the sound of Tenzin's name, Ceba raises her head. She is bruised, and there is something broken in her face, so that one of her eyes is swollen shut. It is impossible, in the half-light, and with her hair hanging dishevelled and matted over her, for Tenzin to be sure just what is broken. He can only be sure that it is her.

At first she doesn't recognise Tenzin. He is just a splash of red robe in the gloom, washed in the flickering light of the dakinis. She shrinks into the wall, hoping that in a moment of mercy, it will open and swallow her.

Then she gasps and says his name, and Gephel hears, even though it is quiet and beneath her choked breath. Gephel leans forward, looking into her face. She refuses to look back at him, and instead gives a single dumb glance to Tenzin.

Tenzin says nothing. There is nothing to say. She is shaking with pain. He feels it, it courses through him.

Gephel straightens, He recognises her now. "This is your one," he says. "I've seen you talking to her."

Tenzin nods. There is no denying anything. Clouds of flies

noisily ignore the dried herbs hung in bunches to deter them.

"I've seen her in the market, as well." Gephel's tone is neutral. He may as well be talking about a yak, or a dog, or a rain front crossing a hill. "I know about this one. She and her sister were there when Seagal Tulku's horse reared as though it was possessed and threw him. He died on the rocks, in front of them."

He pauses, searching the dim recesses of a few hours ago. "There was something about a snake. No matter... Jampa likes her..."

He is smiling, that dark thing again, smiling with everything but his eyes, which are dissecting Tenzin, taking in everything that his brain can process and many things that it cannot.

"No matter."

He steps forward, takes hold of Ceba by both arms and thrusts her towards the table. "Here," he says to Tenzin, to the room, to the jars and hung skin and boiling bones and on account of all these, also to her, "here..."

And he arranges her, in one strong movement that is part lift and part throw, as though she was already dead, onto the table, and deftly reaches here and there and ties her arms and legs. He finishes and looks at Tenzin, his eyes calm and unhurried.

As for Ceba: if eyes can be numb and feral at the same time, this is how it is done. Part of her is still walking with her sister, laughing, feeling the sun on their backs, and then seeing in the distance the tulku and his party coming into view, on horses ambling slowly along the narrow track. She still feels the sharpness of the rocks as she prostrates herself when the tulku draws near.

Everything since that flick and slither of twisting

serpentine blackness against the rock near her has been a blur that keeps falling in on her. She is trapped, breathless and choking, under a tidal wave of blood and tears and voiceless cries, and everything that happened around her has been one unstoppable, seamless *thing*, with no heart.

Tenzin realises that Gephel has left the room. Somewhere in the last few seconds, the other monk said something. Perhaps it was "I'll be back," or "Jampa needs to get back", or "needs to shit". The details and context are gone, lost in the darkness that Tenzin feels smothering him like earth, like the shadows in Master's room.

He is alone with Ceba, alone with her in the centre of this heartless, seamless thing that has come from nowhere. He goes to the table.

She is not looking at him, she is somewhere else. That distance allows him the thought of her skin being cut, her flesh being torn, of things hard or metallic or stone or unyielding, of things that blind or peel or burn touching her... causing her to recoil like a dumb, low-born animal.

His mind reaches for the quarter of the void from which Yamantaka presides over oceans free from fear and doubt, ripping them apart like sacrificed offerings, Yamantaka who bears garlands of bloody heads torn from bodies born of delusion and grasping...

There is no one to feel fear... there is no fear.... he stops, he exhales slowly, forcing his mind into submission.

The flies have paused in their buzzing. Ceba turns her head towards him. Her eyes have opened, and through a film of something that should not be there and is not quite blood, she sees something written on his face that she cannot decipher.

She sees him look around, and then she recoils again and whimpers as he picks up a knife, the blade and handle of which are covered with blood that is almost dried.

She recognises that he is unsure; she has seen that look before, that look of uncertainty, that doubt, there was something like it on his face that day he almost, she said to her sister later, kissed her. But there was no kiss then, just doubt. And now there is doubt again.

Tenzin is imagining what could happen. He imagines cutting the bonds that tether her. He is gaining control over what is happening, over what he is thinking; over his breathing, for it is upon his thinking and his breathing that it all rides. He will get her out of here. It will all have to be done quickly. If Gephel returns, he will deal with Gephel. They will run.

He slices through the leather thongs. He lifts her quickly and carefully to her feet, supporting her limp body, pressing his bloodless face against her throat.

She finds some resolve, and lifts her head, and both her eyes are open now, and she lifts a hand to his shoulder, as if to help him take her weight. And he turns to the door. They will run.

And then none of that is done. He is looking down at her, still tied to the stone table.

"I am here, Ceba," he says.

He hears Gephel reenter the room behind him.

Compassion for all beings rises in Tenzin. It is a bell pealing above the clear ground of emptiness. The unconditioned nature of all dharmas, of the aggregates known as Tenzin, as Ceba, as Gephel, as Master — at last he sees their essential natures.

He knows what he must do.

As he reaches for the kartika, and waits for Gephel to join him at the table, finally he understands compassion, and the thousand fists and eyes of Chenrezig close forever.

All that the Thunderer wrung from thee
Was but the menace which flung back
On him the torments of thy rack;
The fate thou didst so well foresee,
But would not to appease him tell;
And in thy Silence was his Sentence,
And in his Soul a vain repentance,
And evil dread so ill dissembled,
That in his hand the lightnings trembled.

— *William Shakespeare*

In a post on the edge of the Empire
where the paved road gives way
to rough and dangerous paths
and wilderness, savage, untempered,
home of centaurs and shadows;
in the dark marsh beyond the wall,
lies movement...

The guard's heart jumps,
his eyes start,
not from fear, for his flesh and will
have been tested and are resolute and strong;
but from the certain realization
that what slopes,
rough and loathsome,
what lopes through the darkness
towards him is Norwegian.

ALL THAT THE THUNDERER
WRUNG FROM THEE

HE CAN JUST MAKE IT OUT. There are wisps of light forming in the sky above him. He can see the spreading clouds of doubt and confusion that the Norwegians have left in their wake overnight.

He turns his head — what an effort it is now; things are torn that should not be torn, dislocated that should be well located. The sun is lifting itself over the horizon. Its temperature as it rises is violent, its colours are chaotic; everything it touches becomes terminal.

The star pauses in its progress, sending shadows fleeing from the crucified pilot. They are dark knives, they flay all that they touch as they slide towards the coming day.

With light, the fear that has been circling beneath his pain eases, it breaks the surface to breath. It is a sea monster, all gore-flecked teeth and writhing flesh beneath dark scales, the aroma of death sweet on its breath.

Nothing as bad as he feared.

His flying suit lies scattered and torn into pieces on the ground before him, where it has been left it to taunt him, to confirm his shame and the inevitability and rectitude of this situation.

The twisted span of fuselage to which the Norwegians have chained him stirs, its broken shafts and splinters of steel and wood wresting his body, puncturing his skin, forcing his limbs into positions that channel nothing but breathtaking pain. The chains and wire they have used slice into him, an endless outrage of steel against flesh.

Things have been better.

A clockwork child stirs on the ground near his feet, waking where it went to sleep when the sun set the previous evening. The creature's metallic skin crackles under the weight of the gathering day, expanding as light enters it, finding its familiar corners, opening its secret rooms, the tide of photons reseating consciousness in the springs and coils. The child's gears click into life, the flesh within them quivers as the mechanical blood moves.

Despite the pain, the Pilot feels his head clearing, the memory of the things that filled the night abating.

Through a break in the cloud above him, the bulk of an airship is visible in the palm-sized absence of darkness, a patch, a black silhouette sliding behind the clouds.

The airship has spent the night floating above him, immersed in drifts of barium, long-chain polymers and desiccated blood cells. It is the master of his predicament.

*

Predication: firstly, the Pilot has been fastened by his superiors, the Prelates, for punitive reasons, to the exposed spars of a crashed Norwegian airship, deep in the territory of the rebellious and all but uncontrollable People of the Clock, as they call themselves (or simply 'The Clock', as the Norwegian Union insists on having it, so that there are no individuals, just a nameless, amorphous thing); all while a pacification — which is to say, a spiritual exercise of great urgency and with appropriate consideration of pressing exigencies well beyond the pale — the object of this being the subduing of the People of the Clock — and this is proceeding; a great cleansing; a reducing of the landscape to a Norwegian certainty; the removal of all impediments to Faith, the subjugation of the Clock.

Secondly, the reason for this Predicament: he has been accused, quite accurately, of treason, of showing compassion, empathy and understanding for the Clock, of failing in his duty to destroy them wherever they could be found; of allowing their couriers and agents to escape through Norwegian lines, and even of passing information to them; in essence, of aiding the enemy. There is, naturally, only one sentence for crimes such as these.

*

And so here he is. Death has been denied him. It gathers around him, its cold fingers playing, but it is constrained from striking.

The Pilot sees a row of glinting lights on the horizon, followed, at intervals marked by the mechanical and regular breathing of a group of Clock people constructing something near him, by the growing, in size and number, of that row of lights. Within seconds, it is clear that they are in fact the mirrored shields of sophistic convenience being held aloft by phalanxes of Guilt-Consumed Repentants (being the three Regiments of the Middle-Eastern Death Cult), all united in the Holy Theological War on the Clock.

The Clock People are active now, but do nothing in response to the approaching Norwegian forces. Those that were building the thing near the Pilot have completed their part in the process. Their creation stands aloof, its sentience forming under his gaze It is learning and assimilating with each moment around it that slides into the next, a collection of gears and coils and levers that, the Pilot sees, is now building itself. It is an intricate blur of motion; countless tiny arms and articulated limbs building smaller versions and parts, which then build smaller versions and parts, and so on, and on; an endless vortex of furious creation and perfection.

The figure takes on more and more shape and form; that of a human, becoming a haze of irresistibly fast, perfectly focused motion. Suddenly it stops, as if it has encountered some immovable procedural obstacle, some issue of mechanical protocol without a solution; and for the Pilot, and the gathered Clock People, who are now thousands, and the approaching Norwegians, and the irrational sky above, there is a sense of stillness, and waiting.

The dark shapes of the Mayan 2012th Squadron fill the air. The buzzing of their comparative pluralistic dementia is deafening. Their bay doors open, talons release from hulls adorned with the remnants of skulls and the vast teeth of jungle beasts, all pulsating thirstily. They let drop their payload of twitching, freshly slaughtered corpses, harvested from the endless stream of victims that pour down the steps of their temples, freshly heartless, sacrificed to eternity.

As each body drops, hooks and whips and blades of holy intransigence lash at it, the tails of stingrays, the flailing of the eyes of peacock feathers; all together they flay the skin from it. Each body becomes a bare, cadaverous, bloody length of nerve tissue and flapping tendons that slips like a pine seed through the air, down to the fields and hillsides below where the People of the Clock, now fully awake and aware, see everything.

As the falling sacrifices approach the ground, the futility of being seen by the Clock People so late, too late to save them, ignites them. In a dying moment of rage they burst into flame, consumed by grief and inevitability, consumed by not being saved. Falling stars, they drift slowly towards the ground, a soft rain of candelabras of grief and tears.

The insatiable roar of the rituals that bore them emerges from the buzzing of the Mayan 2012th. It is a brave and jubilant sound, that rises above the scene until it reaches the ear of a pluralist deconstructionist post-modernist from the Theory Department, who writes a transcription of these very events down on his stomach. He spends the rest of his days in an erotic state, admiring his own calligraphy.

One of the Mayans, a priest who tore the hearts from his own children to gain the right to do just this, breaks formation and descends, weaving his way through the shower of noise and burning bodies and floating ashes. The righteous blood-soaked feathers of his headdress engorge, displaying proudly his connection with everything, the importance he accedes to non-judgmentalism and the value of cross-cultural relativism, as he reaches down with a long claw and slices the Pilot's torso open, from the base of his throat down to his sternum. With his other hand, the Mayan reaches into the Pilot's chest and pulls away a handful of liver.

The Mayan throws the organ into the air. A flock of Pedants and Sophists swoop upon its effulgence of blood and heat, tearing it apart with their tiny, pointless beaks. Each one could do nothing, but together, through the infinite weight of their numbers and the endless noise of their debating, and the unquenchable avidity of their convictions, they rip the liver into half, then into quarters, then into eighths, and so on, and so forth, until finally, there is a piece so small that nothing at all can be done with it. They rip that into half, and begin again.

*

By the next day, the airship has descended to a point directly above the Pilot. A golden thread, as thin as the logic of a Zionist apologist, descends from its empty belly. At the end of the thread a priest sits on a throne, surrounded by a bench in the form of a disc around him, so that he protrudes through the hole in its centre, disgustingly like a terrible lingam, a shrivelled phallus, a parody of rectitude and purpose, surrounded by the vulva of his lofty intention.

"My son," says the Prelate as he draws near. "Your sins are most grievous, and you cannot be saved. Your condition has been ordained, from the beginning of time. Your fate lay down with you when heaven and earth were created. Only now have we realised it, however," and he reaches down with a long needle and a few yards of rough sailmaker's yarn, and begins to stitch the Pilot's torn flesh back together.

As the erupted edges are pulled back into place, they repair themselves, noisily crackling and gurgling to the accompaniment of airship engines and the roar of the 2012th.

"You are not to die, you see…" the Prelate intones. "You are to be repaired and made whole — oh, the things we can do! And as soon as you are healed, and right as rain, and bright as a button, we will take enough liver from you again, so that your situation may serve as a good example. And then we will heal you again. And so on. And so forth. And that will be your existence, for as long as it serves our purpose, my son. God be with you."

*

The pain has eased. A goddess, or some similar creature, came from the airship during the night, and pretended clever sympathy as she removed the stitches.

The automaton that stands beside the Pilot moves her limbs and inclines her head, curiously. She ticks a type of approval at the easing of the pain, but her springs had recoiled, shrinking from the approach of the goddess. The Pilot has seen this, and he knows not to trust the halo of divine light, the soothing words, or the soft touch.

The sound arises again. A buzzing, the raking of talons across the sky. They are come again, this time not as Mayans but as Lamas, flying across a field of infinitely unconditioned and empty dharmas, leaving divine garlands and skullcups in their wake, a horde of enlightenment. One of them descends to the Pilot, who regains consciousness to see the Gelugpa abbot already feasting on his liver, drinking his blood from a skull torn from the corpse of a Clock Child too young to understand the healing power of religion.

The wail that escapes the Pilot is so deep as to subsume the oceans and the skies; there are no words.

The Sophists and Pedants eat their fill again.

*

"We do not care why you told. But who did you tell, and what did you tell? Everything is emptiness, compassion for all beings..."

And the Lama, the Dalai as it happens, slices a stubborn piece of flesh out of the way so that he can finish his stitching. He tugs at the yarn, sees that his work is good and that the flesh is holding and healing already. He looks at the Pilot, waiting for an answer to his question.

The Pilot meets the Dalai Lama's gaze and says nothing.

"Who did you tell, and what did you tell? What do you know? What are they planning? What do they want?" The Dalai Lama inserts his most enlightened finger, the one trained between bloody stones and young thighs, into the Pilot's wound, exciting as much pain as he can.

"Do you want to keep your eyes, your hands, your skin? We do a special little number with hamstrings," he says. "You can trust me. I am but a simple monk. Now speak."

The Pilot says nothing. He is resolved now. Through his pain and because of it; around their torture, and above it; he will be the thing that breaks the Norwegian agenda against itself. He has wrapped himself around the clicking machinery of the Clock woman, the automaton that stands near him.

The Dalai Lama sees it. He feels failure dimming the aura of his reputation; he seethes, and riles, and shakes. His composure and anger reel against each other. His hand trembles as he folds his yarn and returns his Very Special Ceremonial Needle made of a Young Girl's Loosened Inner Thighbone to its place in a Very Special Ceremonial Box made of a Slightly Older Girl's Skull, and returns the box to its place in his Awfully Special Ceremonial Tantrically Evolved bag of Skilful Means, Artfully Crafted from the Flayed Skin of an Infant.

His dignity restored by these Objects of Power being in their Tantrically Appropriate Places, he tugs at the rope on which he hangs suspended from the Norwegian airship. On the ship, the detachment of the Braindead that had been playing cats' cradle with the rigging grumble and leave their game to pull and heave, and groan in salivitic concentration. Over the space of a few hours of chanting and discourses on impermanence, the Dalai Lama ascends, leaving the Pilot alone to heal in peace.

*

There is silence, in heaven and on earth, for three days.

*

The eagle of heaven forms.

First there is nothing, then there is something that arises from itself like a goddess rising from a lake. A single feather appears, full of perfection, with that perfection painted in detail on every surface. Then finally and instantaneously there is the eagle, the will of heaven. Its eyes are fire, its feathers sheaths of flowing lava, its flesh hatred and love commingled. It leaves a soft haze of blood in the sky behind it.

The eagle, the will of heaven, does not circle, or hover. It does not wait, it does not skim the waves of the heights, or hesitate to choose its victim. None of these. It drops directly to the Pilot, talons of diamond and steel tempered in magnolia breath outstretched, the tearing and breaking inevitable, the rending a teleological certainty, its voice a million-strong choir whose cathedral is the cage of its bones, whose masters are the gods themselves...

The eagle falls, consuming half the distance from the moment of the single perfect feather to the healed and waiting chest of the crucified Pilot.

The likelihood of its talons tearing at his flesh becomes certain.

The eagle descends, and half the distance is halved.

The probability of talons tearing at his flesh ceases to be certain and becomes inevitable.

The eagle descends, and a quarter of the distance is halved.

The probability of talons tearing at his flesh ceases to be inevitable, and becomes ordained.

The eagle descends, and an eighth of the distance is halved.

The probability of talons tearing at his flesh ceases to be ordained, and becomes preordained.

The eagle descends, and a sixteenth of the distance is halved.

The probability of talons tearing at his flesh ceases to be

preordained, and becomes entelechially required.

The eagle descends, and a thirty-second of the distance is halved.

The probability of talons tearing at his flesh ceases to be entelechially required, and becomes the result of careful empirical analysis.

Beside the Pilot, the clockwork figure lifts her arm, and with a hand crafted from infinitely complex variations on Newtonian themes, turns a glass eye to a magnifying lens, which she holds up in front of a telescope, which in turn is prefigured with mirrors that are angled perfectly in their reflection of the colour white and the absolute certainty of discrete measurement. She turns all this towards the eagle, which screams and roars right before her now, where it may well have always been, and as the eagle is taking the sixty-fourth part of the distance between the point of the perfect single feather and the Pilot's chest, and halving it, and the probability of talons tearing at his flesh ceases to be the result of careful analysis and becomes avoidable, conditional, and then the result of supposition and soon, ultimately, an impossibility...

The Pilot sees the clockwork figure clearly now. She is a stream of likelihoods so well and finely placed together that she flows within herself like nothing so much as water across rocks in a sunlit stream bounded by shade at the edges, where the water needs to be kept cool and so there are bushes and trees that shade the water and the gradient of temperature between the shaded portion of the water and the sunlit water is what gives it life and is what allows life, and is life, and there is nothing there to measure or that needs to be measured.

In the eyepiece that she holds, with its perfectly aligned lenses, the progress of the eagle — immeasurable and unquantifiable, reducing and reducing through units of comprehension that cannot be delineated after all — that movement, towards the Pilot's waiting liver, is halted.

*

The eagle does not move.

There is silence in heaven and across the earth. Nothing moves, anywhere.

The eagle of the gods is transfixed, impaled by its own corporeality. It yearns to become again the perfect single feather of lava and light; but it cannot.

It is stopped. The eagle is turned to stone by the gaze of the clockwork Medusa, whose parts shimmer in their movement with a light that pierces like a boar's tusk.

The eagle's beak is about to touch the Pilot's skin, to break it, tear it, revel in blood and gore and ripped organs and divine will and eternal punishment, and impossibly huge agendas and pantheons of birth and maintenance and destruction — but it never will, none of these things will happen, because it has been seen, and the awful beak hovers, and yet irrevocably an infinite distance from the flesh it craves.

*

One week later, a single sound, a voice, a thread woven from fragility blended with shredded dreams, arises.

From a pool of dark water near the Pilot's feet, a choir emerges. Faceless, nameless, androgynous, they form an unfolding flower around a singer, a beautiful youth who sings of the world with a voice that brings tears to the eyes of everyone here.

The centre of the eagle cannot hold. It explodes in a cloud of fire and dust that spreads through the air, until soon it may as well never have existed at all. The eagle is gone.

Where the eagle had been, a single diamond now hangs, suspended on nothing. The clockwork woman reaches for it, her arm stretching to an improbable length, her gears and shafts humming with efficiency. She retrieves the diamond from its place and leaning over the Pilot, places it between his lips, where it dissolves, like a star fallen into an abyss.

The clockwork woman has left his side and advances towards the approaching Norwegian army. As her gaze falls on the advancing Cardinals, they turn to stone. As it falls on the three regiments of the Death Cultists, they become stone. The Comparative Religionists become stone, putty and pumice; and these three natures you may compare at your leisure. The Liberation Theologists attempt a defence from behind parapets built of sweeping generalisations welded together with great meaningless gobs of post-modern convenience, but their efforts are swept aside like eagle dust, and they too become stone. Her clockwork hair writhes, alive, hissing snakes.

In terror, the remaining armies of believers turn to flee, but all of them, except the totally foolish and myopic, cannot resist the urge to look back at their adversary, the advancing clockwork Medusa who can see them to their cores, and when they meet her gaze, they turn to stone.

Only the absolute fools survive; and of them, there is always a superfluity. Unable to conjure the curiosity that would condemn them, they stream away, protected by their unthinking terror. In time, they will find new gods; they always will. At that thought, Heaven and Hell breathe sighs of relief, and the Earth shudders.

*

The singer Orpheus has changed key. He has utilised some unknown, unnamed musical device (it is a device so subtle that it can only be heard by someone listening to music in their sleep, or while beneath someone, or on top of someone — otherwise listening to music is useless). His voice lifts then breaks, then relaxes and bleeds a little. The choir stirs as the waves wash over them.

Orpheus sings of a battle called Salamis, and the chorus around him weep, but they have no name for it, and Salamis and love become one.

The Clockwork Medusa's gaze will not turn him to stone — the Pilot knows this. She gathers close, as if with a confidence or the close inspection of small things, but there is none of that here.

Look, she says, and of course the Pilot looks, because he can hear her now, and even more than that he understands her, because she gave him the diamond which contained within it all the laws of time and thought, and space and thought, and love and regret and thought — not to mention half an eagle's worth of eagle dust. All this is inside the diamond, and now it is all within the Pilot, and the Pilot feels as though it is he that is within it...

Within the Medusa, an infinite number of gears and shafts, of carefully and fully reconciled equations, all in measurable, discrete units, and motions and destinations — all race like planets along their orbits to a common perihelion.

Look, she says, and by now you should not be surprised to learn that the voice of an automaton, when it is created by the closely controlled flow of air over an array of reeds constructed from the fibres of river plants over which the doves of the temples of Baalbec have flown — you should not be surprised, so therefore I know that you are not —

that the voice of the Medusa is the voice of a goddess, not a monster.

So, *look*, the Medusa says, *you are free.* Her beauty, now that it has finished terrifying the Norwegians, is no less; and the Pilot looks down and where his body was broken before it is now whole, and where his hands and feet were impaled, fastened through with bronze and iron stakes, they are now free, and where there were chains, there are none.

But do not move, the Medusa continues. *That would be a waste, it is not necessary. You will just confuse yourself, my Pilot. You are not free here.*

Orpheus is singing an ascending scale, over and over, perhaps Phrygian, perhaps Ionian; the chorus follows.

The Pilot, who for so long has felt nothing but pain and wished only for death, now feels his limbs becoming one with the spars of the crashed airship which has been his crucifix. His flesh is growing into the steel; the steel grows through him. This is his freedom, then.

*

What do you think could have happened next?

Did the Norwegians disappear, skulking off to dissolve into a puddle of unanswered prayers somewhere beneath the only unburned bridge across the border between Norway and Tritonis?

Of course they did. There was never another eagle, nor an attempt at a Dalai Lama, nor even the thought of a reformed Mayan Squadron. Those that were not turned to stone soon fell from the sky because no one thought of them any more; or else, like a *kamikaze* pilot whose carrier has been torpedoed at sea and has sunk beneath waves, they circled and circled, with nowhere to land, until finally they ran out of something, and simply ceased.

And the fools that are everywhere — they wandered, and because they had no one to lead them, they were last seen still wandering, deep in some nameless desert. But do not go near them. There is nothing, in this universe or any other, more dangerous than a fool.

And the People of the Clock built, and built. You should see what they built. That so many shining gears could turn in so much free-willed unison…

And the Medusa watched over them, and served them, and was with them, and anything that would hurt them blanched with terror and regret and turned and ran lest it be turned to stone by a gaze that undid the opposer, stripped it and turned it upon itself like a creature from an afterlife.

*

Thirty three eons later, and all of the Clock's processes and things are finally worn to dust and to pieces as small as the screws that fix the wings of the white ant during its fleeting moments of flight, as small as the knots in the oil-slick dreadlocks of a Venus from Ethiopia.

And there is the the Pilot, with his flesh freed, with the cage of his bones released to the soil, with the life of his veins flowing no longer constrained to his bodily frame, but into the spars that bear him, into the soil, and like a tree that spreads underground, the Pilot gathers to himself the elements that lie unused, pieces of the past of the Clock, and the Pilot takes them to himself, and becomes something new, because once there was the Prometheus who challenged the gods, but now there is the Pilot, who is become as one.

Look, says the Medusa, and she points so that taut cables of intention and measurable will reach from her outstretched hand and connect it with the lake that birthed the young Orpheus.

The Medusa sweeps her gaze across the water. It passes like the hand of a god over the deep, and soon the water turns to life, the granite headstone-smooth and hard, impermeate, the sealed and secret source of Orpheus, the origin of clockwork scales weighing stone doves and their paths and their songs. Time gathers around pebbles here in the depths, it halts, it flows into ratios of gears and levers and torque, it presses carbon into an infinity of diamond, it creates sheer rock faces of will.

The gaze of the Medusa sheers across the water like a hunting bird, from light to dapple of light. Where it touches the stone surface of the pool clockwork fish race below the surface, chattering and clicking, chasing the gaze of the Gorgon, wanting to feel it upon them.

Between them, the one from the one side and the other from the other side, the gaze of the Gorgon and the clockwork fish cut and wear at the stone surface, and between them their appetites slice it into squares and circles and other disturbing shapes, and between them they release the squares and circles and the other shapes, and together they rise into the air, slowly so as not to disturb the perfect equilibrium that subsumes all this, and each piece of the stone surface, each square, circle and other shape soon ceases in its ascent directly below one of the burning souls who have been waiting, suspended in the air, their flames and progress frozen for eons now.

The two opposing elements, the two entities, merge and become one, the fire with the stone, and the burning soul with the surface of the pool. And this union achieved, these new entities descend, floating to the ground in a rain of ash.

The gaze of the Gorgon turned stone to water, and in the surface of the lake is reflected the inner law of everything. The world that is in the surface of the lake is not reflected at all, but it is another world, all to itself, and all itself.

The Pilot descends into the pool, slices through the water like a god descending into a newly created firmament, eager for the touch of it, as heartglad as a wasp of Aristophanes on his way to court. He takes great handfuls of everything. His hands are grown, they have become as large as phalanxes on the ends of arms like trees. The water flows across a forehead as wide and as free of doubt as a canyon, it flows over thighs that reach like bridges across the sea at the edge of the world; it flows around feet as large and as well-situated as the anvil of Hephaestus.

The Pilot sees that he has become his reflection. There is no difference between them. There is no cusp; the water has become like air. The Pilot moves like a god here, and from here in the world which first appeared as a reflection, he can see himself as he is. The Pilot who is still crucified is now the reflection.

And he can see reflected there in the old world, the world of separation, the clockwork Medusa, *ticktocking*, looking up into the sky of the other side, *ticktocking*, her mechanical rage so deep as to be insensate and mindless, and it is turned on those who are fated to see it, who look when they should not.

Here in this world, where there is no separation, she stands beside him, her clockworks and flesh sliding and flowing and working together, *ticktocking* in perfect harmony.

They join hands and arms that are mountains; they join thighs like plains and rivers; they lie on a field of sand and gears and stars, like gods resting from creation.

The people of the Clock here are stars, their lives bright and shining; everything is irrefutable; they breathe and glitter.

Where the Medusa was full of rage that turned the world to stone, here she has wings and the thing that cut into her is gone, evaporated and transcended. Poseidon is reduced to foam, and there is no more anger, no more rage, no more seething behind a mask of grief and hate. Where Prometheus was bound, he now has wings, and he flies, and he sees the untold, uncountable stars, the souls of the people of the Clock are each one a realisation of the perfection of a movement, of an intention, of will, of torque, and of desire.

The song of Orpheus and the choir continues everywhere. Everything that hears it falls into order.

RHAKOTIS

READER, THERE WAS A TIME when the world was covered, in all its length and breadth (and the world is flat; you can trust your senses), by a great dome of ice.

The dome was not spherical; it was elliptical, or squashed, if you preference is for ungeometrical talk. By this I mean that its height at its apex was less (much less, in fact) than the extent of its radius. Or, in non-mathematical terms, it was not shaped like a (very large and translucent) ball cut in half, but more like a (gigantic, divine) teardrop, fallen to earth and with its straining sides held in place by the meniscoid properties of the liquid, and its top thus accordingly flattened by the weight of the whole thing.

I trust that we are clear on that.

On account of the pronounced oblate nature of the dome, the roof that it formed above the world attained a height of approximately twenty *favner* above the ground — and this at the very most. Sometimes it was less, but never more.

This distance was somehow enough to accommodate the tallest mountain in the land. In fact, if anyone were to stand on the very summit of that mountain, and stretched upward, extending his or her hand into the air as far as possible, he or she would then be able to brush his or her fingers across the cold surface of the ice.

Strangely enough, this would have been the case regardless of the height of the individual in question. For the tallest adult in the world, or the smallest child, the situation would have remained the same. How this works is a mystery.

Anything that the inhabitants of the world thought to exist above that height — whether empty sky, or the depths of space, or a wisp of cloud far above a stream on a sunny day, or the sun itself — was either just imagined, or a distorted and inverted reflection of something that did actually exist below, in the world itself. Also, not everything in the world below was reflected in the ice above; only some things were reflected there — otherwise there would just be an unreasonable degree of confusion, a cacophony of things that would leave no one any better off.

This might all sound complicated, but really, it is simple; you must never trust what you think you see in the sky above you.

*

The ice had been in place so long — since the beginning of the world, in fact — that the inhabitants did not notice it. In fact they would not notice it, they *refused* to notice it, even on those occasions when the matter was raised by an adventurous soul who might point at some unfaithful reflection or some trick of the light where such a trick had no business to be. These individuals were never thanked for their trouble; in fact they were oftentimes treated harshly.

At such convocations of intention and temperament as these, the inhabitants of the world would, for the most part, renew the vigour and determination with which they would look downward. They would absolutely refuse to look upward, and would usually wish, silently or not, that the troublemaker would cease, desist, disappear, or just wander off and die in a hole. And in fact, one of these things usually did happen. Ceasing, desisting, disappearing, or dying in holes — none of them were all that rare, as the final fruits of dissent go.

Now, the upper surface of this dome of ice was covered with dust and debris of every conceivable manufacture; dust that was the result of every process that could be imagined or found anywhere, and many that could not. Certainly, the nature of this dust, and the catalog of its characteristics, was sufficient in scope to exhaust the capabilities of — to *outencyclopedia*, if you will — all the encyclopedias in the world, and then some.

To the inhabitants of the world below, it did not appear as dust, of course. To them it appeared as shifting clouds, or flights of birds, or some other variation in light and shade that seemed equally natural and familiar, always certain in some shape or another.

With this mention of dust, our introductory survey of the dome above the world is almost complete; but we do need to make one more comment.

In its construction — and of course we are discussing no ordinary ice here — the dome was infinitely strong. This strength was despite the fact that at its circumference (or the circle with which its lowest extremities bounded the earth, and touched it), it was so thin as to be all but non-existent; this having the result that no-one noticed it.

At its apex, the dome was almost infinitely thick. It could not actually *be* infinitely thick, of course, because that would be a logical absurdity, but we can accept that at its apex, the dome's ice was *almost* infinitely thick; the point of this, of course, being to protect those who exist outside the dome from those who exist within it.

This, in general, explains the occlusion of the sky. It also goes a long way towards explaining why the world is the way it is.

*

Now the people of the city had seen no real clouds for many years. All they had seen were the shifting sheets of dust above the ice which they took to be clouds, but it was all just tricks of light and shade, and there was never any rain.

No rain had fallen, and there was no water in the rivers or lakes or reservoirs. The citizens, both rich and poor, drank oceans of wine and beer, and in addition there was a constant trade in bottled water, imported at great expense from somewhere (no one seemed sure where exactly), and sold at great profit in the markets.

For celestial, and even mystical, reasons, the ice had stopped melting. This was the real reason that there was no rain.

There were young people taking up careers in the public service or the military, or beginning apprenticeships, who had never in their lives seen so much as a single real cloud, and nor therefore a single drop of rain as well. The drought had gone on so long (and no one could recall now for how many years) that no one noticed it any more. When the endless lack of rain entered conversations, it was nothing more than an idle curiosity, or one of those general complaints that are to be had about the world when there is no serious expectation that it will ever be remedied.

*

No one noticed the first cloud that formed, because it was only visible for a very short time. It was absorbed back into the firmament quickly, leaving no trace of its existence.

The second and third clouds were larger and darker and lasted longer, and so after a while they were noticed. By the time the main body of the rain front arrived, rolling down the mountains with cracks of thunder and sheets of lightning that draped across the slopes like white lace, every one in the city had taken to the streets and was looking up into the roiling dark undersides of the clouds as the first raindrops fell.

So this was how it began to rain; and the rain, once it started, did not stop. At first the citizens watched with great happiness as the world seemed to drink for days on end, its waterways and reservoirs filling. But if there were gods to say 'enough', they must have been distracted, or laughing at this, or angry somehow, for the rain continued for days, and then for weeks, without pause, until for every year that the drought had persisted, a week of rain had fallen. And still it came.

Soon there was no more looking up into the wet sky with spread hands and wide smiles; no more children dancing in the rain. The streams that tumbled down the mountainsides had become raging torrents, and there was so much water everywhere and it rose so quickly that finally the people woke one morning and found that the city was isolated, its roads and bridges impassable, and that they were unable to leave.

The city had become a group of islands. It had been sepsected by the water, carved into seven small hamlets separated from each other by dark, unfathomable water that scoured everything with no pattern or sense that could be discerned.

So much of the dome's ice had been melted to create this rain that the light that glowed through the translucence of the dome was brighter and harder, and bluer and whiter. No one noticed, of course. (*cf.* previous comments concerning resolute looking downward, and the consequent inability of most to see the details or true nature of anything manifesting at an altitude higher than oneself.)

After all this had been achieved, the rain stopped in the middle of one night. The downpour ceased in an instant, as though it had been turned off somewhere. This was clearly a night possessed of ontological weight. It had no moon, and so was impenetrably dark and black.

And then, as if everything was part of a conspiracy, no method of lighting anywhere in the city could be made to work. Not a single lamp burned anywhere, everywhere was darkness.

The people of the city waited for the sunrise, but the sight of the fingers of the dawn playing with the dark outline of the horizon never came.

The night refused to end. Some swore that they had noticed that there was a sound of gears turning somewhere far above that had stopped; others were adamant that no such sound had ever existed. (This disagreement between these parties has never been resolved.)

There was no means of contact between the seven parts of the city that had escaped flooding by becoming islands; but what did that matter, really? With no light, existence was precarious enough, without worrying about anything as pointless as the problem of getting from where you were trapped, already becoming inured to the darkness, to what you hazily remembered might be an island somewhere over there — perhaps — from where you could — perhaps — hear sounds, that might or might not be people. Perhaps.

Everything had become *perhaps*. Nothing was certain any more, other than the endless darkness, which had seemed to come from nowhere, but now most certainly was everywhere.

*

On one of these new islands, a baker named Vineleus and his wife sat in their kitchen in the darkness.

A mountain of bread sat on the benches around them. They could not see it, of course; but they knew it was there, because they had baked it all themselves.

It was still there, but everything had changed. The aroma of baked spelt loaves had filled the house before the endless night fell, but everything about it was muted now. The smell was like damp wool, only vaguely sweet, and everything about it was unsatisfying.

Even the touch of the loaves was leaden, as though its very existence was muffled, and when they broke the loaves to eat, the sound of the crust tearing was muffled as well, as though they had cotton in their ears. It was, they agreed between themselves after long hours of thought devoted to the matter, all very strange, in that perhaps kind of way.

But as for the taste — when had bread ever tasted like this?

It was like no bread they had ever eaten, and on this they were of one mind. It seemed musical; and the music caused them to see movements of light in the darkness. The taste, its perfume and the feel of it, it was all orgiastic; the experience was, to be polite about it, most definitely total.

Never had the act of eating had this effect on either of them. So Vineleus and his wife had food, and this sustained them, totally, and in a kind of light which had nothing to do with the endless night and the monsters outside.

Outside, the darkness gathered in pools at the bases of walls and in the twists and turns of streets and alleyways. It leaked in under the doors, it gathered in windows and then eyes, building up relentlessly, about to put everything away forever.

FEEDING THE BEAST

ONCE UPON A TIME, there were two people. If you know anything at all about them, then that is enough for you to know the beginning, the end, and everything of our story.

And if that were the case, we would just as well end this right here; but I do not want that, because I have an agenda that would not be done to its end if we stopped here; and so we are, you and I, going to proceed on the assumption that you know nothing about these two people, and the thing that they created.

And as for my agenda; if you know what it is, then you are right to know, and if you do not, then that is a good thing too.

*

These two lived in that world which we all secretly know to be the real one; it is the world in which every single thing is made from an idea; from the notion, or the supposition, of something; and where in turn every idea, every notion, and supposition, without exception, is realised as a form; and so the idea is made as a thing in the world.

In this way (and this has never changed) the world and its ideas seem always to be joined somehow, and required of each other in some way, as if they are each the high and the low at the same time; or as a pair they are the interior and exterior of each other, and each can really be measured only against the other.

But this kind of thinking is unnecessarily complicated, and if you wish, you may regard it as mere metaphysics — or even worse, a cosmology. And we do not need to concern ourselves about these things, for such thinking has never achieved anything. And so, let us return to reality...

In this world, they both, the man and the woman, lived in a town that sat on the edge of the sea, on the curve of one of those bays where the water — forgetting the state of the tide or the strength of the wind or the phase of the moon — wraps high around the foundations of the buildings that crowd the edge of the sea.

No-one in the town — or most other places, for that matter — knows even the slightest, inconsequential thing about the sea, let alone anything of consequence. But we two, reader, you and I, are in a privileged situation, for I know a little about the sea, and what little I know, I am about to share with you.

*

Here is the sea. Even though its waters lap against the docks and the waterfront, the feeling of familiarity that comes with this proximity does nothing to lessen another sense; the sense of a darkness that moves slowly in the depths, like drifts of great shadows with flickering, sparkling edges that flash like stars behind the clouds of storms, and these sparks in the depths rise to the surface in great slow upward waves of light, repelled by something in the dark depths, something heavy...

To those who look only so far and too cleverly, and then too cleverly suppose that the surface of the sea is just the surface of the water and no more, these sparkles of light are nothing but sunlight, reflecting myriadly off the breaking surface of the water as it shifts and rolls; but they are not that, at all ...

For the sea moves, ponderously in its depths, under its own weight, and across the weight of the earth, so that the masses move hard and slow against each other, and there is a massive weight, and there is no room for anything to form, for here is the engine room of a chaos, and it is the chaos which drives everything. And it is this chaotic darkness, where everything is crushed so finely that nothing can exist, which is the engine behind the sparkling lights that cover the sea like an endless, restless, cloak.

When it is a dark night, and when the sky is covered with clouds so that there is no light from the moon or the stars, and if there is a heavy rain falling across the surface of the sea — when those things happen, then there is no swarm and chaos of lights on the surface, and everywhere there is only darkness.

But this is neither an atmospheric condition, nor is it a matter of reflection. The depths of the ocean have paused, for reasons that it would be pointless to enquire into. The engine rests, mysteriously, and there are suddenly no points and stars of light which flee like little satyrs from the depths to the surface.

And this is why the surface of the sea can be so dark and black at night, when there are clouds and rain; it is because in the depths of the sea, everything is paused, and chaos is resting.

The truth of it is this; all things draw their life from these engines, in the depths of the sea, and also in the depths of the Earth. And that is why no one can understand the depths of either of these things, for to do that would be to understand the depth of things and of the world, and who can understand the world? It is a mystery, as it should be.

And so, I am not telling you this to try in myself to

understand the world, or in the expectation that you might understand the world. This tale is more specific. And it is not even about feeding, or beasts, or the feeding of beasts in general — it is about the feeding of a particular Beast, and its endless particular hunger, and here is a picture of the Beast, to save you the bother of imagining it.

Of course, there is some artistic licence at play here, but the representation is true enough to the essence: this is the Beast, the feeding of which is our primary concern.

Now, let us approach the matter.

*

Through the town, there was a river that flowed to the sea, and the man and the woman lived on opposite sides of this river. Although they had both noticed it, sometimes as a sluggish, listless stream of no particular importance, and sometimes as a torrent that was almost wide and almost raging, and had even broken its banks on occasion — although they had both noticed it, they had only looked at the surface (and I have just described how the surface of things can deceive...); and they had not wondered about anything beneath that surface, for its depths have never been found, and cannot be contemplated, for the river is part of the sea, and by now you know something about the sea, as we have made a beginning of that...

It was said that the river was as deep as the world itself; but who knows? I do not, for I have never seen the bottom of the river, or the bottom of the world, for that matter. And no plumb line has ever found the bottom of the river, and it is common knowledge that it never will.

Near the centre of the town, on the banks of the river, there was a maze of tunnels and buildings all thrown together, and intertwined. Tall walls and underground curved ceilings twisted around and back upon themselves, and here the inattentive easily got lost, and everything was made of old brown bricks, so that the effect, in general, was of the earth, and age, and of things being solid. In the middle of all this construction of bricks and earth was a long platform of black stone. It was more ageless than old, and it sat next to the rails that connected the town to the city. It was here that the people of the town came when they travelled to the city.

The man and the woman had never spoken. But things changed at 7:49 on the morning of an ordinary, mild day, when no one was thinking anything at all about seas or rivers, and they seemed some unimaginable distance away, and of course there was no idea anywhere of a Beast, or indeed anything Beastly.

She was ahead, and he was slightly behind, and there were others around them on the long platform of black stone, a quietly intent group about to board a train, and in that moment, she turned and handed him a piece of fruit, cut from a larger piece. It was a small piece, of no special consequence, shaped like a casual word or two, a passing thing, and nothing was unusual, except perhaps this one thing: that if there was a day on which there was suddenly a new idea in the world, a day on which our Beast was born into the world, this was the day, and here was the birth. It was a new thing; but it was nothing unusual, in itself.

From this moment, everything took root and grew, and it grew slowly at first, but it grew easily. In the shadows which formed where they met (and having now met for the first time they kept on meeting; for a genie had been let out of a bottle, and it was a very clever, resourceful genie, who had seen enough of the insides of bottles...) — wherever they met there grew small and delicate bushes and shrubs, which shimmered in a silverlike way, and they grew, in size and in number, so that at first there were just a few, and then soon there were more, and more, and so it went on.

In what passes between people, there is never any stasis,

117

for that is death. Every piece of fruit passed between people has something that grows or lessens in it; and this is what grew between them. On the branches of the plants, there began to grow a new kind of fruit, something fleeting and subtle, as if it might not expect to last. And if the fruit was not plucked, then it would soon fade and disappear, as if it was made of ghosts. But when it was plucked, and shared; then somehow it became real, and the man and the woman found that there was pleasure in the fruit and in the sharing of it.

But there was something else, a third thing, that was plucking the fruit, feeding on it. There was a form, a glimpse of something among the shadows, more of a disturbance in the light than a thing, really; it was a shimmering, in some kind of darkness; or at least that was how it was in the beginning.

Of course both the man and the woman noticed it soon enough; even though its movements were small, and it was young; it was not grown yet, just for now it was the size of a child, just a *putto* of a thing, but they would notice the flash of light in the shadows, or even just a kind of rush or presence in the passing of a moment, when it would seem to them that there was something alive there, something that was smallish and seemed to live on the little silverlike fruit, and was playing with them. And as the plants and the fruit that they bore all grew, so did the thing which lived on them, and it was soon obvious that the thing was a creature, of a quite specific and individual kind.

And the creature was never far from the plants on which the fruit grew, the fruit which the woman and the man passed between each other frequently now. Soon they realised that the creature would eat nothing else; it would eat only the silverlike fruit.

The weeks and then the months passed, and the plants and the other things that grew in the shadows kept growing, without seeming to need any more attention than just that; just their shadows, as the man and woman passed.

First the plants, silverlike, with a light that seemed to be within them, grew to be almost as high as our two were; and it was all in some way familiar up to that point. The plants were pleasant, and in some way familiar; but they did not stay familiar, and they kept growing, and soon there were trees taller than any person, and larger, in a way, than life, and some of them even seemed to be like those oaks that are centuries old and can seem unimaginably large, even like the ancient oak in the town's park.

And then they each, in their own time, realised that never before had they seen trees as big as these, with such broad and tall canopies; nor had they tasted anything quite like the fruit that grew in abundance on the great spreading branches.

And the creature was no slouch; as fast as it could eat, it grew, and there were times that it seemed like the trees, to have become larger than life, but that was only sometimes, and there was no pattern to this, certainly no pattern that they could discern, either of them. And since they were both the kind of people who like to discern things, and thus have a measure of them, this caused them concern, and increasingly they thought about it, and increasingly they were frustrated by it.

There were other times when the creature seemed to have become small, or farther away, or somehow both, but it really, for both of them, was impossible (or at least too difficult) to say whether the creature really did change in size from day to day, or whether it was something else, altogether, and not about size.

And to confuse matters more, there were days that they felt as though the creature had gone, or even that it had never been there at all, as though they had imagined everything, all along. And they were both unsure, unsure perhaps above all else, as to whether the creature had noticed them.

They had, when they had first seen it, thought it to be a charming little thing, a kind of a pet. At first it had run about, childlike and gambolling, small and pale, on its two feet, fluttering its wings uselessly, to be admired in a light kind of way, and playing with its tail like a kitten or some other baby animal which will most likely not last through the spring; such is the light grip that young animals have on life, which of course is why they should be admired as quickly as possible.

That now seemed a long time ago, and because they had seen it almost every day, they had not noticed its growth. And now, suddenly, the creature was large and could stand over them, and seemed as though it might cover them with its wings, which were large and shot through with many colours; and the fact was that it had become a Beast now...

The shadow that it cast was sometimes alluring and inviting, and could have something gentle about it. At other times, it seemed as though there was a darkness in both the Beast and its shadow which was dangerous, and might swallow them; and then its whole darkness made them feel unsure, and nervous in their stomachs.

And there were days that they felt that the Beast was staring at them in an implacable way, standing right in front of them, like some sphinx, mysterious and inscrutable, demanding all their attention and all their answers, demanding fruit, demanding everything. And whenever they gave anything to each other, the Beast would feed, and grow larger, as if the fruit was meant for it, and as though this was the only, inevitable, way of things. To feed the Beast.

In this way the Beast grew strong. At times it was like a storm that would blast, and cause everything to reel as though it might fall apart. And then they both became afraid of the Beast, for there was a kind of careless tyranny about it, and it began to follow them everywhere, and it would block their view and their paths, so that at times, it even seemed that there was nowhere to go but towards the Beast, because the Beast was everywhere.

They even tried to reason with it, each of them talking to it separately, when they were alone; they told it that it could not be part of their lives, for while there was something so very familiar about it, there was also something very strange; but the Beast would hear none of it; it could hear nothing, it seemed, but the growls of its own hunger... it would lower its head, which had grown impressive now, and they could see into its eyes, which burnt with a flame that was always there, which were always strangely a heated colour, the colour of a strange flame that seemed to have no particular source, in a way that made them feel uneasy, that seemed to heat the blood, and live in it. So now there was a fire, to do with the Beast, in their blood.

And sometimes they felt as though they had lost control. They were in control of things and themselves most of the time, for that was their nature; for them to know their situation, to know their own lives — but here they were, with a monster that filled their eyes when they looked, filled their ears when they would hear, made their skin race with anticipation when they would feel touch, and they both would sometimes find that the knowledge of it would sit on their tongues like an ox when they tried to talk, and so there came to be many things between them which were thought, but not said, because of that ox, which was large, and heavy.

Both of them felt an exhilaration of freedom, but it was only the breeze of it, as though it was from a distant place, as though they were on some shore, and the breeze was coming in off the wide sea, and carrying with it the scent of a distant land, exotic with spices, and fragrant with the aroma of forests, and mountains, and deserts with caravans of great animals crossing them, laden with trade and adventure, and the noises of great new cities and light rolling across the plains and hills like great herds of unknown creatures, and more great creatures with scales of gold and feathers the colour of the sea, and the creatures fly high in the sky and build nests on the peaks of the tallest mountains.

And the only way to get there was somehow the Beast, for all the breeze carried was a hint, not a promise of anything. They felt as though the Beast, if they allowed it to, would take them away, on some adventure, for its back had now grown broad and its wings had grown strong and wide, and its fur and scales had grown dense and strong.

But at the same time there was an enclosing, as though they were trapped, and unable to move. They had the feeling of a freedom, but they also had the reality around them of being unable to move. But it was not the Beast that made them feel trapped; for the Beast, with its faraway, burning eyes seemed to tease them with a kind of release, but it was a disturbing release; and in a way it was against them, for it was they who were trapping themselves, unable to move in the strangeness of their town which had become a world now of uncanny shadows and spaces, a world of trees laden with wonderful and mysterious fruit, all presided over by the Beast, which could now be everywhere at once, and nowhere all at once.

And so they reached a point which seemed to be inevitable, and their fear won out, and they decided to deal with this once and for all, for they were both sensible people. They would get back to their lives, they would free themselves from the Beast, and they would free the town of these shadows, and the impossibly big trees which obscured everything, hung with the strange silver fruit; they would free themselves from all of it.

And so they were disconcerted and confused, but the man and the woman decided that they were resolved, and they would be strong, and so they stopped looking at each other.

But the Beast did not leave them alone, for it was always hungry. It would not be denied.

*

And so away from the town, among the dunes, they built a wall around some flat sand a few steps from the water's edge. They built the wall as quickly as they could, but it was so tall and required so much deliberation that it took them an entire morning to do it. There are some things that take real time, no matter how quickly you do them.

The wall was made of rock, in pieces lifted up from deep beneath the sand. Each one was lifted by a single thought. Some thoughts are easier to have, and therefore harder to use properly, of course, so for the first hour or so, the results were patchy; there were rocks that were too large, and weighty, and these took a while to find a use for and they took some effort to move, and sometimes they would even not work at all, and had to be discarded, but this is the way of construction, and cannot be avoided. Some were smaller, and these were more flighty, quick thoughts, and these were useful for filling the gaps between the larger thoughts. Some were flaky and weak, and could not be used at all, because they fell apart. This is the way of construction as well.

By lunchtime, the wall was finished. They had made a prison. The job was truly impressive; the wall was higher than they were, and to get the rocks up to the very top of the wall, some of the thoughts had had to be very lofty indeed.

After lunch, which as always they ate separately rather than together, because that was the right thing to do, and which therefore had a vague hint of something unsatisfactory about it, they applied a finish, a veneer, to the wall. Their words poured smoothly, as though it was easier now that a plan had been agreed to; here was a project that they could sign on to. Their words filled the gaps in the wall, close to exactly, and then they glazed over the new surface with periods of silence and some nods and acquiescences.

Then the woman and the man gathered together the fruit from the silverlike trees, which were now large enough to touch the lower reaches of the sky, and which were everywhere through the town, and they were also everywhere along the beach, and these trees had shaded them while they had built their wall.

The flesh from the fruit of the trees they mixed with words and pauses and other pieces of silence, and the resulting mixture, when it had been applied to the wall and had dried, was wonderfully smooth, and mirrorlike, and shining. It was bright and reflecting in the sunlight, like a mirror, with nothing rough or reckless, nothing that a Beast could possibly get a foothold on.

Here was what they had intended. A prison, in which to keep the Beast confined forever, away from them, away from anyone, where it would disturb no one.

There was a gate that they had made to be an entrance, and it was very strong, made of resolutions cross-braced with the best ethics. It was all joined together on a framework of practicality, supported by arches of the hardest, most appropriate logic available. It could be closed and sealed in several dozen different ways, but opened in only one.

And that one way was so deep and uncanny that they were not sure, day by day, that they could remember how to do it, because to open the gate required a key that could be made only by giving something up, and they were sure that they could not do that.

*

And now they had to be sly, for the Beast was no slouch. It had shown itself to be single-minded, but it was far from stupid.

And so the next day they deceived the Beast. Using as a pretext the firmness of a promise based on good intentions wrapped in a half-formed hope and tied up with unsatisfied yearning, the three of them went for a walk along the edge of the sea. It was all innocent enough, near the shallow water, well away from where the ocean floor drops away into the measureless abyss.

On their walk, they came in time to their great construction, which had taken them until a lunchtime to build. There they casually and distractedly led the Beast through the great gate, which glistened now like a mirror in the sunlight.

Now, here is a most curious thing. If all that you have read so far you have been somehow expecting, as if it has been some almost familiar tale unfolding — then this next development is perhaps something that you will not have been expecting. Here is what happened next.

When they entered through the gate that sparkled like

water in the sun, into the enclosure of the smooth, mirrorlike walls, they found that during the night, observed only by the light of the moon, there had risen from deep in the sand more walls, held together by a mixture of things which were then and remain now unknown, and uncanny mysteries; for these were thoughts that no one knew.

These new walls had not risen to any kind of pattern, and that made the maze that they formed all the more a maze. There were passages, and dead ends, there were loops and bridges and tunnels, so that a confusion could somehow cross over another confusion, and create a strange kind of order that seemed immeasurably greater than just a solitary mystery. This was the character of the maze, and before it they were suddenly dumbfounded, and the ox was back on their tongues.

They did not enter far into it. At the first corner, they paused, suddenly afraid, as though the maze could somehow block out the sun, and everything might become dark. They almost touched each other in a kind of panic (and they had never touched each other) and their nerve was almost lost, but they had a plan, and they would stick to it. And quickly, without another word with which to feed it, they hurried out and left the Beast there in the maze, and locked the great gate using bars and nails and great bolts, and they covered it with beams and sheets of the hardest iron, made of the coldest promises that they could find.

In this way the gate was sealed, and the Beast imprisoned.

*

There was no howling, no protest. From the moment in which the gate was locked and sealed, a silence fell heavily, like a dead bird, as heavy as the albatross falling from the sky, and suddenly everything was different.

In the silence, with its dead weight and its hint of dust, something seemed to vanish, for a time, and it was a relief, and so the man and the woman resumed the routine of their lives.

Everything was familiar again, but it was a familiar shell. There were no shadows, and there was nothing disturbing moving in the corners of their sight, and even the trees shrank and withered, for the Beast, you see, was locked away in the maze down by the edge of the sea, and everything, it soon became obvious, had come from the Beast; there was something about the Beast that was behind everything.

So everything was familiar again, but there was now a strangeness, because the Beast was missing.

*

Now, there were those in the town who had begun to notice what had been happening, and the three of them — the man, the woman, and the Beast — had become, in a few select circles and among those who somehow, for whatever reason, felt it to be of concern to them, or felt it to be business in which they were involved or *should* be involved, or were thankful *not* to be involved — the three of them had become famous, famous in that small way that requires talk and muttering all delivered with a disapproving sneer, or a sniff, because some things cannot be said plainly enough, and can only be sniffed at, because once something has been sniffed at, there is usually nothing else to say.

It is fair to say that when the Beast disappeared from view, there were sighs of relief, kept politely under various breaths and sniffs, in these various quarters. After which the chatter stopped, and a few pieces of fruit that had been turning poisonous on the lowest branches of the silverlike trees fell to the ground, where they decayed into nothingness in the space of a minute or two, unnoticed.

*

After this, the man and the woman did not meet, or even see each other, for many months. They lived their separate lives in the town, and the town was happy enough to keep them apart.

*

But few things can be sealed away forever, and there came a time when something came back; it was the shadow of that feeling that had been such a new and curious thing when the Beast had first arrived.

Inside the maze, the Beast had stirred and opened its eyes, and the thing that was different now was different below in the ground, and above in the sky, but nothing could be seen, it could only be felt, and because nothing could happen, and only be felt, everything was constrained; they could not be friends, although they had it in them to be very good friends; and they could not be lovers, although they had it in them to be very good lovers. Instead, they were forced to be strangers, for that was all that was allowed to them by the world.

But whether you are allowed to do something does not always matter, even if it is the world that is doing the allowing and the not allowing, and so it soon turned out that it had become too late for the man and the woman to be strangers.

Around them, no-one seemed to notice. Everyone seemed happy with the charade. It was like a play, with the two of them pretending to be strangers, from a distance, pretending.

That was enough to let them off the hook with the town, for now.

*

One day, a feeling of unease circled about the man and settled on him, and it seemed as though the birds in the sky might close their wings and cease to fly, but then still stay suspended up there; and the creatures in the sea might cease to move and swim, but remain suspended in the water, as if in a sea of glass... but despite the feeling of unease, everything kept moving in the sky, and also among the trees and also in the sea everything kept moving, and on the face of it everything kept on as normal, even though a difference was there; and the difference was that everything was uneasy, and wrong.

Now, the man knew that the reason for this uncanny state lay sealed inside the maze, behind those walls — this development was, he knew, to do with the Beast. He knew this as he stood before the wall, which was long, and high, and had become dark, and offered him nothing; and directly in front of him was the great gate that had stood unopened for so long, sealing the Beast in.

Now here is what happened.

As the man stood with the sand and seawater shifting around his feet, the birds in the sky paused as if they were in some shock. They stopped in their paths, and then moved, and then paused, and then moved, and they kept doing this; a stopping and starting that went in short uneasy motions; and yet this somehow seemed normal, and in that, it felt right, it felt somehow as if it was the correct order of things.

And whenever the sky froze — and soon he realised that it was the substance of the sky that froze, not the birds, although the effect was similar — then, the waves of the sea would likewise seize, and the water would immobilise to glass. This all happened in the pulses, the spasms of movement, and between them he saw the great gate swing open, by itself, with no-one there to open it, and it opened in the same short, uneasy motions, and this was a curious thing, for the gate had been sealed and locked well, and yet here it was opening, and it was all quite inexplicable, but somehow quite normal at the same time.

And so finally the gate stood open, and the pulses of movement and stillness had stopped. There was no movement from inside the walls, and everywhere was silence, but it was a more natural silence now, not the uncanny atmosphere of the preceding minutes, when it had seemed that everything had become sculptural. This silence was just the simple lack of movement, and behind it, somehow accentuating it, was the low and distant thrumming of waves breaking in the distance, and water was rolling on the faraway parts of the sea; and there was another murmuring sound, closer, and that was the waves breaking on the beach nearby.

So, it was with a deep silence accompanied by the calls of circling gulls and the sandlike hiss of waves collapsing and disintegrating — with all this existing as a kind of commentary, he entered the gate.

The maze was larger than before. It had grown, extended in all sorts of directions. The walls had become bowers heavy with growth, so that the maze was now adorned with flowers such as he had never seen before; these were something new, entirely. In bunches, in sprays, or singly, they hung suspended in the foliage that grew and moved, they hung like jewellery on the dresses of women at a dance. And the flowers seemed to recognise him, or at least to acknowledge his presence, for as he passed them, they shivered slightly, or turned as if the better to see or hear him.

The maze had become bigger than seemed possible, bigger

than could possibly be contained within its walls, and the more that he saw of it, the more he saw the impossibility of what it had become. It was something of a miracle... the corridors were wide in places, as wide as one of the main streets in the great city of the interior where there is no sea and the sun never sets or rises; and in other places the way had grown small, so that it was almost impossible to find, and even more impossible to pass. In other places it had grown over, and the foliage curved strangely over, growing up and together to form a roof, with strange white trumpet-like flowers hanging down thickly, so that he sometimes had to fight to find his way between them, and the thick tendrils clung to him, and gave way only grudgingly, because everything was out of control, and wild.

At the end of a great corridor, in a court, near a *cul-de-sac*, just past a bridge and opposite a cave, he finally found the Beast. It was curled around the base of a great tree which was sterile and bare, for it had no leaves, or flowers, or fruit; it had only dark and bare branches.

The Beast was as large as it ever had been, but it was sluggish, as though it had woken from a deep sleep. It had not been fed, so it had not grown, but neither had it withered or died — it had only slept. And the truth of it occurred to him; that the Beast would never die. It could not die.

The Beast raised its head in his direction. Its fur and scales were dull, but alive; its wings stirred so that he imagined he felt the air move from them; it looked directly, purely at him, a blank, pitiless kind of summarising of him, with eyes that had only thin, moonlike crescents, slivers of white, and many stars in them, and apart from that were nothing but discs of ebony.

And that was enough for that day.

*

The next day he returned, and standing before the Beast, he found a seed in his pocket. It had been with him since the day when the woman had given him that piece of fruit in the middle of that quiet crowd at 7:49. The seed was from that first piece of fruit, and he realised now that he had kept it with him always, and actually had never forgotten it at all.

At the sight of the seed, the Beast started. It threw its head forward suddenly, and when he knelt and pressed the seed into the soil (for it seemed somehow obvious and beyond question that he should do that, here where the soil was deep, and rich, and fertile...) the Beast opened its mouth and let out a hungry call.

It unwrapped itself in a smooth motion from the trunk of the tree which it had been guarding. It came gliding as smoothly as a thought over to where he stood, and there it stopped, coiling with an excitement that was somehow dumb and single-minded, in a pile before him, like a spring somehow wound, yet still lithe and loose, and relaxed; as if it somehow had great power in either state.

And then leaving the seed in the soil and the Beast attending it, he left the maze, with its wide and narrow pathways and its fruit hanging strangely like trumpets, and he returned to the town which now seemed to be less interesting, and if anything a little smaller than its size suggested it should be, and from then on, something of him always stayed there in the maze, with the Beast.

And when he returned the next day, the maze seemed even more wondrous than before, and now it was so large that it took him the entire day to find the Beast. But eventually there it was, lying with its long body wrapped three times around a tree which had grown up where he had planted the seed. Already the tree bore fruit, and there was a clarity about it, in the way it was shot through with a particular shade of blue that was the blue of the sky and the sea; and each fruit shimmered with a sound, and when he drew near he heard the sound to be a word; and it was just a single word each time, and it was a different word for each fruit. And there were so many that the effect was complete; it was a complete language, all of its own, an entire language spoken at once.

As for the Beast, it was dozing contentedly, full of the fruit it had eaten. Around it lay husks and shells, and skins and seeds. Its fur and scales had a shine to them, it was a healthy, energetic shine, and the rise and fall of its ribs was sated, and even.

A breeze blew in from the sea, making the flowers shake so that separately each flower made a note, and together the sounds were soft and deep, and there was a great sea of notes. Not all were in harmony, because there were so many, there was an almost impossible, irrational number. But also because there were so many, the effect overall was a harmonious one, and so the sound of the wind through the flowers was a great, complex chord.

The sound of the flowers grew suddenly louder, and with that the Beast became disturbed. It stirred and looked in his direction with eyes that were blank and as hard as black stone. Whatever it was that the Beast meant, there could be no question about it. Whatever it was.

He was caught by surprise at this change of mood on the part of the Beast, for it had become serious, and he quickly turned away and fled along the path back to the gate, where anything, it seemed now, was able to enter and leave the maze at will; anything, that is, except the Beast. The Beast followed him to the gate, snarling and snapping at his heels, jumping this way and that, always seeming about to lunge and bite, but never quite doing it.

The Beast worried at him, but did not strike, even though it was riled. At the gate, it would not cross the threshold. It was as if something invisible restrained it, as if there was a leash that it strained against, and it stood in the gateway, barking its strange call, its large wings flapping furiously.

As the man walked away from the beach towards the town, with the Beast remaining in the open gateway, its agitation subsided and the creature became wistful, or nostalgic in advance of some future or other, and there was something resigned there as well, as though to something lost, and because of that it paced, cowed, just inside the great invisible missing gate, as though it was still there. And it paced, and kept pacing, and would not rest.

"I have had it with this Beast," the man thought to himself as he walked, and he swore that he would never return to the maze and its churlish resident. The Beast could look after itself; let it starve, if it meant that.

And with that he returned to his home in the town, where at least there was no confusion.

*

And his resolution in this was so strong, and unwavering, that he did not return to the maze for seven whole days. It was only on the night of the sixth day that his curiosity at last overcame him, and underpinning this curiosity was a kind of affection diffused throughout him, for something of the Beast had a foothold in him now, and it felt all the more disturbing because the feeling was new, and there was something exhilarating about it.

And so on the dawn of the seventh day (which was a spring

day, and fresh and brisk) he came back to the maze and he returned to the tree that he had planted, but the Beast was nowhere to be seen.

The fruit (and there was truly a great deal of it) had been eaten, and the remains lay scattered around in a great disarray, but of the Beast, there was nothing.

The spring breeze had stiffened. It whipped at the sand, and the hedgerows stirred and shifted. Across them rolled waves of colour, alternating not in time with the breeze, but endlessly changing to a rhythm that had some other, stranger, source.

And so on the seventh day he wandered abstractedly through the passages of the maze, and there were many new paths and dead ends and intersections and tunnels that had not been there before. During the seven days since he had been here, everything had grown in complexity and size, so that even the things that were familiar had a kind of newness about them. And as he explored, all the while searching for the Beast, he was accompanied closely by the strange wind which stirred the masses of the hedgerow.

And then he came to a corner that was new, where the ground seemed unsure and became like sand, shifting under his feet, and the hedgerow had grown even more dense and entangled in itself, so that the foliage grew dark and mysterious and heavy with deep shadows, and the only directions in which it was possible to see at all were along the paths of the maze. It was as though the maze was playing the game harder, now.

He wondered on all this briefly, as he stood there, but it was only briefly, for his attention was really on the tree that had appeared before him.

This was not the tree that had grown from the seed that

he had planted — no, he had not retraced his steps, coming back to where he had started from. This was a new tree entirely. A second tree.

The flowers which covered it were new altogether, and while his tree, the tree that had grown from the seed he had planted, had a silver complexion, with something blue in it, or with a wash of blue over it or suspended somehow between the tree and himself — this new tree had a redness to it, and this colour seemed to flow from within it, in the way that seaweed moves, so that the tree seemed to undulate in some tide, far distant and yet at the same time here and close, as though there was some uncanny gap that the apparition seemed to bridge, and as though whatever it was that gave this new tree its redness arose from itself, ceaselessly. The tree, arising from itself. The tree stood unmoving except for this undulation and its seaweed redness.

And there was something that stirred, in that movement beyond the breeze, somewhere in the air or in the light, which began to cause a stirring in the flowers on the tree, so that they seemed to ring with sounds that came from the depths, all at the same time. So everything was part of something else.

Around the red tree, resting in a bolus of young branches and foliage tangled near the base, the Beast lay reclined, relaxed, as if in a moment of rest, gazing out of eyes that were languid and the size of serving plates. It seemed to recognise him, and in its gaze was a certainty, and he knew that the creature had been waiting for him; and that it had been knowing, with certainty, that he would arrive. And he also knew that it was waiting not just for him.

There was something so familiar in this, the dark density of the maze, in this tree with its red waves stirring, in the flowers that sang like trumpets in the uncanny breeze, and finally in the blank, ceramic gaze of the Beast; there was something definite and familiar in it all.

And there was the thing that was missing.

And just as the man realised that something was missing, the Beast unravelled from the tree, and slipped down from the tangle of branches in which it had been resting. As it moved, there was something in the angle and the aspect of its back and its path, and in the reflection of the lights of the tree on its scales, and something in its look, that all together brought to him the sure knowledge that this tree had also grown from a seed. And in the same instant, he knew who had planted it.

The Beast had been eating from this tree as well, that was clear, and it had grown. It could rear now, upon the coils of its tail and its haunches, and as it reared in front of him, it was close enough for him to feel now the heat of it, and its teeth almost brushed over his skin — and then it looked him in the eye, and it saw into him.

He was stared down by all this, and averted his gaze, and in that action there was a glimpse, off somewhere at a distance, of some colour and movement, but when he looked, there was nothing, and the flash of colour and movement could have been anything, or just an impression.

He found this all disquieting and unusual. He swore again, irrevocably, that he would not come back.

*

The next day, he was back, and he stood before his tree, and he went to the red tree, which he knew of course was hers, and there was no one to discuss *that* with, and the Beast was to be seen nowhere.

*

And now the waiting became endless. There was the waiting, every day, for the time (and it was a precise time which never changed; it was 7:49) at which he could travel down to the beach, to the maze. And once he was inside the maze, then there was waiting again, but this was the active kind of waiting. It was the time that it took him to find the trees, and so he had to move, for they seemed always to have moved, and always the Beast was near one of them, grown in size, and also grown in life and in vitality, so that its presence was becoming in a way physical, and rough, and at times uncouth, which of course can be fitting and appropriate for a Beast. It was a rude strength and a rude vitality, and it was hungry for life.

*

And now the Beast, though it nipped and harried at him, and spoke strange speech in some language of its own, had become familiar, as a friend or a family member or a witch's cat might become familiar. And he had come to find the Beast's attention pleasurable, so that he even relied on it somehow; and soon he found that it was essential, and this was certainly a surprise. There was a level on which the Beast seemed able to break through anything.

That look that the Beast gave him, with its wide, black, eyes-like-saucers; that uncaring, knowing look in which so much rested, and there was no labour, just something like a god. No one, nothing else, looked at him like that, and it seemed to see all of him, and yet it responded to nothing, and so there was something about the Beast that was absolute and changeless.

But where the Beast was changeless, the maze was not.

One day, all the fruit of the two trees was gone, stripped away, and the leaves also were gone and scattered, so that the trunks and branches were bare, and had become a great tangled mass of branches, with that internal shadow inside themselves, and their branches were like arrays of some kind of aerials.

Of the Beast there was no sign. But there was a sense of it in the air, and it was also behind the air somehow, and he imagined that he heard its call and its movement, and when he stopped and listened closely, and inwardly leaned in towards the sound, it did not dissipate, as fancies do when they are inspected. The more he listened, the more certainly was it irrefutably there; in the distance, and yet somehow all around; a playing sound, as though the Beast was sporting in the nearby shallows of the sea.

As to *which* sea, well, that was impossible to tell, for by now there were several oceans in the maze (admittedly they were smallish ones), not to mention a few decent-sized lakes, at least three mountains, some hills and forests, and a desert or two. And so there were many shorelines and shallows in which a Beast might sport.

And now, apart from the presence everywhere of the Beast, and the pregnant state of the flowers, and the base, stark state of the trees, and the sound of the sea which was somehow everywhere and behind everything, and the maze itself, there was nothing.

In the silence which underlay all these impressions like an impenetrable, clear ground, the man now stood still, and he became silent in himself.

And now nothing else happened until some plants had begun to grow up out of the sand and wrap themselves around his feet and between his toes, and then nothing more happened until some tendrils from the hedgerow had tightened themselves around him, and then even the rays of the sun, normally pencil-like and straight, curved as they came near him, and they took curved paths around him. Nothing else in the world happened until all this had come to pass, and he was covered with all sorts of shadows.

And now this next thing might seem strange, and not at all what you might expect; for time itself had been doing something unusual, and now it was about to stop altogether. It seemed as though the sun might begin to go dim, not as it does when the night comes, but somehow in itself; and it was with this realisation that he stirred, and shook himself; and he resolved that if nothing was endless, then this was no exception; and so he resolved to explore the maze properly, and to see what he could find, so that it would not seem endless.

He would find the Beast properly, once and for all; even though it was here one day and gone the next, and it seemed so unreliable and self-inclined. And he would solve the riddle of the second tree, and its provenance, and he would solve the riddle of her and her whereabouts; for all of this had become a sphinx with endless riddles and questions, and the sphinx stopped him along every path.

*

Here is an aside, reader. Some explanations require a great amount of time — so much, in fact, that they never resolve, and are never complete.

It is as if a sailing ship is crossing the globe, trying as hard as it can to complete the circumnavigation, but the globe is growing, as though it is breathing and taking in air like a huge, inflating balloon, and there is always more distance to travel, so that no matter how it struggles and strives, the sailing ship can never complete its voyage, for there is always more. Nor can it turn back; that would do it no good at all, for it could never regain its home port, for the reasons just described. And so just as surely as it could never reach the far side of the world, it could also never return home.

But if a globe that is forever expanding means that the exploration can never be complete, then the opposite is true; a shrinking, collapsing globe will bring the exploration to its conclusion all the more quickly; for the distance to be travelled is always, continually, less.

What happens when the globe collapses suddenly? Not in any sort of predictable, orderly fashion, but in an unexpected instant... The voyage of exploration is suddenly over, perhaps even before it began, and the mystery, if there ever was one, is resolved, and any voyage by our ship is not required; in fact, it is impossible. All this can happen even if the voyage has not yet begun; and the end result is that the exploration and the subject of the exploration are suddenly one, the problem and the solution, the seeking and the goal — all become one, in one inexplicable, mysterious synchronicity, which is not just coincidence but something greater, in which nothing makes any sense at all, but even so is uncannily in the right place.

*

The preceding about ships and globes and collapsing is to explain how it came to pass that once he had stirred from that stasis that had seemed endless, that had been on the verge of going on forever, he soon afterwards found a particular room which was at once in the maze and in the town. He found it suddenly, out of nowhere, which was passing strange, because it had been there all along, in both places, with its great white walls which rose above everything that it contained, and which seemed more solid than everything else. (How a room can be in two places at once, I leave for you to ponder.)

It was in this room that the synchronicity was done, it was achieved and sealed. They saw each other. In that room, in that minute, the globe of the world collapsed into a kind of single point with no height or length or width, and that particular voyage of the little sailing ship was suddenly, instantly, and undoably complete.

This happened among a crowd of people, and they were all from the town, yet none of them noticed anything, for the mark of the Beast was not on them, and there was nothing of the Beast within them.

And as for the details of how this came to pass, and how there was a synchronicity involved which would cause the earth and the sky to pause if its inner workings could only be understood — we are going to omit those, because they could never be more than suppositions and hypotheses, and the mystery there will always be unscalable and complete. That is the nature of synchronicity; to be a mystery, and more than just a coincidence.

*

Now everything was different. Whenever they were together, and that was often, and words passed between them, the Beast was there, with its ceramic gaze that missed nothing. And everything they said fed the Beast, and the man did not have to search for the Beast now, because it was always there, eating from their hands.

Now it is a strange thing that when the town spoke, its

words would either evaporate into the breeze meaninglessly, or they would fall to the ground like lead weights and sit there, glinting in a useless and dull kind of way like dead fruit, so that the Beast would not even glance at them. It would even go so far as to turn its head away, so that its gaze was averted in some kind of deep melancholy. With its rear legs, which had great strong thighs like a gigantic insect, like some kind of mantis, and which dug into the ground like pylons carrying some electricity of life, it would back away, leaving the the leaden grey words to rust away; and in the night air, under the moon, they would rust and crumble, so that by the morning, when the sun rose over the sea and cast long shadows over the maze and the town (for they had somehow become one), the leaden fruit were always gone.

In the end, as soon as the town began to speak, or even look as though it might speak, the Beast would shrink away, and would have nothing to do with it.

And the Beast never left the two of them, either when they were together, or apart; they began to feel as though they were always together.

As for the times and places that they met, this was left to synchronicity, which has its own timetable and will be neither rushed nor denied, and so it happened frequently sometimes, and other times seldom; and sometimes it felt as though it was not part of any pattern at all. But there were other times when it seemed as though there was an underlying pattern, certain and complete, somewhere a plan of things, and times, and places, and their meetings were somehow part of that plan. But the fact was that none of this made any sense to either of them. It was all nonsensical.

Sometimes it was as though they were struggling, pushing against a tide. But sometimes there was a tide that they were *with*, not against, and then they were with a great primal flow that seemed to emanate from the vast and mysterious machines at the bottom of the sea and in the deep parts of the earth.

And in that primal flow the Beast was with them always, in its unpredictable, unknowable way.

*

The maze now seemed to change every day, so that doorways or gateways would appear or disappear, or dead ends would come to life somehow, or some whole new section would open up. The maze had become so big and rambling, so like a mansion with an impossible number of rooms, that there seemed to be a whole new world appear in it every other day. A hill might become a mountain, before his eyes. A depression in the ground could fill with water and become an ocean, complete with a distant horizon and sea monsters that might come from the depths to play, all writhing and jumping in the foam.

And all this time that the maze grew more wondrous, the town became a paler shade of grey, as though something in it was being drained of life. Everything had become perfunctory, as though it was a machine or a habit, just filling up space, and everything else had gone to the Beast, somehow.

The Beast was now very broad and strong, and its eyes, which were now like great black dinner plates, saw everything, near and far, without delay or qualification. Everything was reflected in them, because they had become dark mirrors, holding within themselves first all of the maze, and then, it seemed, all of the world.

*

Now the game had changed again. Now the words came thick and fast, and the Beast ate them ravenously in big, hungry, gulps, plucking them down from the trees or up from the ground, taking them quickly before the town might stumble across them, and not knowing what they were, might mumble to itself about the words without understanding them. And as if they were some strange, exotic fruit, suspecting that the fruit might be poisonous, the town might be shocked or left speechless by the words because it did not understand them. And then the town would be left breathless, and grey.

Here is how it would often work when the town would overhear a word that had passed between our two, and see it hanging like a ripe fruit, or even if just some unsure echo might be heard; then the town would feel a self-righteous kind of stiffening, with a garnish of indignation, all at the recognition of that forbidden, archaic scent which was food for the Beast, but anathema to the town.

And there was so much of this indignation that they soon felt, the man and the woman, that the trees had become too heavy with fruit, and too large. They felt this not because of anything in the trees or in the fruit; they felt it because of the indignation. The song of the flowers that hung always heavy towards the earth was deeper, and it was louder. And as it became louder, they became concerned that it would attract the attention of the town, and if they really knew a single thing about the town, it was that the town did not approve, and would never approve.

Even so, even with all the talking, the man and the woman had never touched each other, in the presence of the Beast or otherwise.

And all of it, the colour and the noise and the chords and

the trees, and the Beast, with its great pelt and scales that caught the light like stars, and behind everything the endless silence — all of it hung over the town like a strange, colourful, quilt.

By now the Beast, and the trees, and the hedgerow and the maze — everything — had all grown so large that our two sometimes had the idea that they should rightfully be afraid, and because ideas are what they are, they each had dreams that were unsure and senseless and restless, and there were dreams of the size of things, and foremost among these things was the Beast; for the Beast now towered over them, so that sometimes it almost seemed to shelter them, and it could leap vast distances and scale great heights within the maze, and both of these things it did for sport, and enjoyment.

Its muscles rippled in the sun like water. Its wings flamed and shone in the air, iridescent like a butterfly's, and it was an iridescence of colours that shifted upon themselves, and flowed upon themselves. There was a sense of fascination there, as if the Beast was some kind of kaleidoscope.

It would swing its long tail carelessly back and forth, or its wings would flap, excitedly, as if it was anticipating something, or it might swing its head, and its mane would fly out wildly. In this way it could, at any moment, suddenly bring down a wall of the maze, and this was the reason that the maze was always changing, as pieces were removed or moved or turned on their heads. The man and the woman both realised now that this was how it had always been done, this was the only thing that had changed the maze, ever; it was always the Beast who changed everything.

On this particular day, the Beast leaped up from around one of the trees on which it had been feeding, its great legs propelling it faster than a thought, and it ran along a length of the maze, crashing into the walls and hedgerows, swinging its tail and taking down into pieces what the crashing bulk of its body spared, so there was suddenly noise and chaos and destruction everywhere, and where the length of the wall fell to pieces, a new place behind it was opened up and revealed, and they saw it, and the Beast watched with approval as they went into the new place that had been opened up for them.

And this was always the manner of the Beast now, to be chaotic like this; and so there were always new places for them to explore. And of course they knew that this was the only way in which the maze had ever changed, and secretly, they were in awe, they approved of the strength and roughness of the Beast, and they wished secretly that everything was more like this.

And still there was never any touching; they had never touched at all. In all of this, the only thing that had ever passed between them was words.

And then a letter came.

*

Elements in the town had been noticing things, and it hardly need be said (although that will not stop us) that the town was not happy with these things that had been noticed.

In fact, the town, as a whole, was worried to distraction, a state to which it was well suited. And as well, the town had become occupied with the thought of all the things that had *not* been noticed; and because those are the worst of all, the worry about what *those* things might be had brought the entire town to a state of apoplexia.

When the man and the woman met anywhere, there would always be talk between them, for when they spoke it was easy and they could achieve anything, and they had become easy with each other. But this easy talk was the very thing that the town had noticed, and it disapproved, and it muttered to itself in a voice that was like a desert choked with its own sand. And from behind that voice the town looked at them, with eyes that had something of a dust storm in them, and below that look there was always that same sneer, always there, so that nobody could miss the point; the town did not approve.

He found the letter pinned to the door of the maze, in a brown envelope, where it could not be avoided. The letter was both general and specific at the same time, for it was easily long enough to be both those things, and several more besides.

The letter did not mince words; displeasure and moral outrage fermented in every line, and there was a luxurious amount of those. The man and the woman had been far too public and shameless in their talking; and what would people think; and who knows about this; and what would those who do not know think if they *were* to know; and of course think of the children, because even the children have noticed.... apparently, there were many things to consider now that the town had been outraged.

Especially when the town, in the heart of its suspicions which it voiced without restraint, was right. This sense in which the town was right would make the man and the woman both lower their gazes sometimes to the ground, which is where you look when you are thinking too much about the inside of your own head, and in this case that was certainly true, and worst of all, they began to care about what the town thought. That was the beginning of a kind of slavery.

But for the Beast, this all meant nothing. It did not care who was right, or who was wrong, or whether anyone was a slave. The Beast made sure that they kept meeting each other, and it was chance upon chance, for to the Beast synchronicity is just a simple, basic thing, like breathing air or lapping up water. The Beast lived simply and brazenly in their thoughts, and it gave them dreams, real dreams that you have when you sleep, not the pretend ones that distract your waking hours, and it always lured them back to the maze, where it would sport with them, and amuse them, and worry at them. And more and more often it would take on a form that was bigger than everything, and somehow behind everything, like a source, or a shadow. When it was like that, it would take over their senses, and overcome them.

But if the Beast did not care about the letter, it must be said that the man and the woman were affected by its judgments and its vitriol, all of which had been applied with a fine brush and in great, painstaking, detail, so that its purpose was plain, and clear, and dripped from the pages, and could not be missed. And so in consequence, every notion that they had and every word that they said came to be overlaid with the town's disapproval, which was easy, because there was so much of it about, and the sneers and looks wore away at them, in a way a little like a sickness, but more like a plague of the undead, so that everything was threatened by a sickness of doubt, and there was a kind of vague fear that poisoned everything.

But the Beast kept on in their blood, and it recreated the maze every day until eventually its passages and paths were unrecognisable to anyone other than the man and the woman.

To them, it always had a familiar air, even though it was new every day. And there was something about it which was inevitable. Everything was inevitable.

*

It became normal for them to see each other in the maze, now.

It was just the Beast, breathing. And always, there was the sound of the sea behind it.

*

One day, finally, there came a day when one of them touched the other on the hand, and how the Beast liked that!

And then the next day there was another touch, from him, and then she touched his arm as they left each other on the day after that. These were only small things, but they felt somehow important, just as it had been important for so long that they had not touched. That they had talked so much, but never touched. But now things were becoming different.

When one of them kissed the other on the cheek, lightly, as they were leaving each other, and the Beast was there in the aroma of her skin, that became another of those things that the two of them were so good at; things that there was no going back from.

They never went back or turned away from anything, in the end.

*

The Beast was spending its time relaxing, sunning itself, which is to say that from its point of view everything was plain and simple, and the fruit was sweet and plentiful, and the maze changed by the hour, and walls fell and rose, and the sound of the sea was behind it all.

The Beast had grown, and there were times that it seemed to be the largest thing that there could be in the world. Even as big as the world itself sometimes. And so despite the town's apprehensions, the world was good.

*

One day, a wall fell down when the Beast breathed near it. It happened at the exact moment during which the skin of one of them brushed against the skin of the other.

The room that was freed when this particular wall fell was a particularly open one, and filled with a bright and clear light, and it was endless and open in all its dimensions, and the things in this room were without number, and the light that was in this room was not the light of the world, but the light of another, larger place.

They had both arrived in this room together, and they knew without saying anything that if they were free to choose anything, that each of them would choose to be here forever, and this was all because of the third thing that had grown up between them, in the domain of the Beast; and it had been well fed by them, even though they had tried to starve it to either death or good manners.

But the Beast would have none of either death or good manners, and knew only how to be fed, and they really, in themselves, knew nothing any more other than how to feed the Beast. Feeding the Beast had become everything.

Now, a citizen of the town had happened to see the skin of one of them brush like a feather on the skin of the other, and this citizen had recoiled in horror and indignation, for here was a crack in the aether, and through that crack was a glimpse of that endless room that was so well-lit.

The citizen ran indignantly to spread the word, so that decency might prevail, so that what is appropriate and acceptable should be done, and this outrage of touching skin was most certainly none of those ... this would require much more than a letter.

As the man and the woman stood and talked in the maze, unaware of the consternation gathering in the town, the

Beast watched. Its eyes were dark pools with no limit to their depths, just as it is with the sea, for there is nothing that can reach to those depths of the sea.

The citizenry was mobilised now, and its anger had been stirred. They came chattering in a febrile mass, and as they arrived, all the walls of the maze fell together into the ground suddenly, and everything disappeared in a second, as though it had been only dust all along.

And just as quickly as it fell, something else rose up from the ground in its place. The thing that rose from the ground was as hard as granite, and as it grew it gathered the citizenry up with it, and it formed an amphitheatre, with rows of tall seats that rose up and away from the centre, and it was not long before all of the town was a mass, all seated and dappled with shade cast by the bare branches of the trees which had lost their leaves.

Ten thousand citizens of the town had gathered, and they yelled and complained to each other, and each of them held a copy of the letter in which all the things had been documented and said, and they waved the letters aloft or held them to their breasts, or kept them concealed in their pockets, and they were all exclaiming at once, so that the air was full of words, and all of the words were used to prove all the others correct; so there were endless circles of words.

And now everything was in the plainest sight. The centre of the amphitheatre was as big as the world, and its noise and confusion was as big as the world also. The man and the woman stood together in the centre of it all, with only bare sand beneath their feet and the bare sun above them, and there were only the trunks of the great trees near them, and the trunks were all that was left of them, and they had begun to wither and die, for they were burning from the inside, and with every word that rippled though the crowd, the thing that was burning in them burned more.

A drift of ashes had gathered, and there was a silence between the man and the woman, where before they had talked so much.

There was nothing that paused now, there was no strangeness of time, no stopping or starting of skies or birds. Everything proceeded, one thing after another, one wave after another, so that there was an order to everything.

Their hands no longer just brushed against each other then moved apart in that quick kind of way. They held firmly, and there was something in that that no longer cared about the town, or the letter, or the amphitheatre rising to obscure everything. They did not care any more, in their hearts, what the town thought. And in their not caring, the coliseum that surrounded them had become a fragile thing, barely able to support the weight of the town and its words.

The Beast was there, pacing back and forth. It towered over them as though it had been built by something that was itself uncanny in size, and it watched them intently, and it ignored everything else.

The man and the woman ignored the crowd, which was rattling and stirring and breathing gasps of horror, and everyone — the man and the woman and the crowd all together — was so intent that no-one noticed that the sea had risen steadily, that the waves were pushing and eating at the foundations of the amphitheatre, eating at it from the outside, so that it began to crumble, from the outside inwards.

Between the man and the woman it had become like this; there were no words now, because they did not need any. The thing that was between them was in the blood, so that they felt as though they were with each other, together on a field that had its own kind of geography, unique to itself. And this was not an emotional thing; it was in the blood, beyond anything to do with individuals, and it was quite archetypical, as though they somehow lived in a land of large and perfect things, and this was the geography in which the Beast brought them together. It was a geography of the blood.

In the convolutions of that geography, the town would have seen coincidences; and there would have been many, but they would have been disconnected, and so to the town they would mean nothing. But the man and the woman had long known that there was something that came from the Beast and also from beyond the Beast, and that something was a synchronicity; it was how everything was connected. And all the synchronicities were signposts and markers on the landscape that the Beast had created.

And this was all the landscape into which the sea was rising, pouring into the amphitheatre, and the structure was sagging and crumbling, and falling in on itself.

The Beast blocked out the sun and the sky, and it was breathing over them, and from it dripped the darkest sea water that there could possibly be. The Beast, with its dark, endless eyes, leaning over them.

And now direction and gravity began to tilt, and the man and the woman were leaning against each other, and for the first time they felt the warmth of each other, and this was when they leaned all the way, and kissed. There was nothing else that could be done, it was inevitable.

This was also the moment when the weight of the sea came into the amphitheatre, and it fell apart, for the structure had been nothing more than sand all along. First the entrances and then the rows of seats collapsed. The water into which the citizens of the town fell in a heap was raging and swirling, as if it was in chaos to its depths.

The waves brought with them creatures from the sea. They shone and sparkled and flashed, and their backs caught the sun as they broke the surface upwards, and then downwards. They were marvellous monsters, each one unique, and they called out, each in its own tongue from the deep, and somehow the man and the woman knew that the creatures were calling the name of the Beast. Which was something they had never thought of before, as a mystery or otherwise — that it might have a name; but now it seemed obvious.

The days of the Beast's youth were over, it was no longer a pup. It was now grown and ravenous and wild, and ready to eat the world. It stood on its hind legs, and its tail thrashed among the waves, its scales flashed chaos and sunlight, its fur was drenched and hanging down, and water poured down from its mighty flanks and neck.

The Beast bared its great teeth at the man and the woman who were holding each other in the swirling waters, surrounded by the creatures which had come up from the sea. It lunged, like a wave with all the weight of the sea behind it. And in one easy, single motion, as if it was water, the Beast took both them both up between its jaws.

Then the Beast leapt into the water, the length of its body crashing with a great noise through the waves.

All the creatures of the sea followed it, shrieking and calling, and there was a raucous procession away and into the depths, and the shock of this in the water was such that the last pieces of the maze, and the amphitheatre, the theatre of it all, gave way and it all slid into the water, like a mudslide, suddenly with no form, so that it all ceased altogether to exist.

The citizens of the town were aware again of nothing but the town, and they were happy, for everything was suddenly in order again, and the Beast, which had been the cause of so much confusion and unhappiness for them, was gone. They stood up out of the water, spluttering and simpering, and for a moment they stood unmoving in the subsiding waves and the receding water, and then they shrugged their shoulders, and muttering and grumbling about the first thing they could think of, they turned towards the town, and they all went there.

And from that day on there was talk of how the Beast and its creatures had torn apart the man and woman and dragged their bodies in pieces into the sea where it consumed them, and so the sea and the Beast are to this day the enemies of everyone.

*

As for the Beast, it was never seen in the town again, for it had returned forever to its home, which is at the bottom of the sea.

And the sea was deeper than anyone knew, and there the Beast ruled its dominion; for all along, the Beast had been the ruler of the sea, the ruler of all its breadth and all its depth, and everything in it that moved.

And in the depths there was always light, for everything there was radiant in itself; and there the speech of all creatures was in accord; and the Beast ruled with its great eyes like black wheels, and its scales that were rainbows, and its appetite for all the fruit in the depths of the sea was endless.

And there the man and the woman live to this day, and nothing in the kingdom of the Beast has ever cast any shadow, or darkness, or any other thing against them, ever.

THE SERPENT & THE HORSE

IN LAKE TRITONIS THERE ARE TWO ISLANDS. They are Phla and Mene, and they are set like a pair of jewels on the water, exquisite and many-faceted on the pale skirt of the great wide surface of the lake. They are jewels, in a field of blue and green.

Phla is the home of daemons and forces, and the energies that lie behind things, so that everything on Phla is to do with the depths of the lake. Phla is dark and blinding, a wild, unruly place, and we are not going to deal with it here. It is too big. We are here for other reasons.

As for the island of Mene, though, we can begin to understand it. At the time of the events which combine to make our narrative, it was covered almost entirely with the city of Tritonis. Its countless buildings were spread around a thousand grand squares and a thousand wonderful gardens, or they were arranged along countless boulevards and avenues, each intersecting others constantly, so that a map of the city looked just like a grand mathematical diagram of some complex, geometric place. A kind of sacred geometry, instilled into a place.

Everything in Tritonis, every building, every bedpost and desk and silver ring, was finely worked, with wonderful craftsmanship and attention to detail, so that in its placing every object was exquisite and finely ordered, and the entire phenomenon was set like a priceless, many-faceted jewel on the gown of a finely dressed woman, and she was the lake, and the shore, and the land, and it had all gone on forever, like a mountain does, sitting on the world like a great slab of time.

The city of Tritonis was enclosed by a great wall, and it was as old as the island itself, and it was as thick as the city's forum was wide, and as high as one of the minarets in the city. All that meant that it was very high indeed, and so the wall had never been breached, nor had the moat before it been crossed, by anyone, ever.

Now, there was just a single piece of the island of Mene which was not covered with buildings, and this was on account of it being outside the city wall. It was a rolling field of grass and trees under a great blue dome of sky, and it was bounded on one side by the city wall, and on the other by the shore upon which the waters of the lake rose and fell, all pushed and pulled by the moon (and the moon is not to be trusted, but we shall not go into that here).

This field was the home of many creatures. There were some that stayed, some that came and went, that flew, or burrowed, or crawled or hopped, and among them all, there was a horse, and the field was her home as well.

The horse was small, with delicate hooves and a long black mane that she would throw and swish in the air, and how the air liked that; and the horse wore silver and feathers because silver and feathers liked to be worn by her, and she set them off well, so that they were never so beautiful as when she wore them.

The horse spent her days roaming freely, galloping in the sunlight across the hills and among the trees, enjoying everything that came to her, and going wherever her spirit led her, into dark places and into light places. And there were creatures that circled in the sky above, riding the invisible currents on great wings, and they talked to her, and the paths that they made and the tilt of their wings created a kind of sculpture in space, as though there was a great spirit there in the sky above her.

But because there was so much, every day, there were times when it all felt like a kind of maze — the island and the depths of the lake, the untrustworthy moon, and the city, and the wall and the field, and everything — until it was a wonderful maze, and it was huge, in that way which scares some creatures, and makes them afraid, but for the horse it was just the wonderful nature of everything, and not something to be scared of at all. For there were many things in the field, and each one was its own thing; the way it sat in the light, and each thing also had its own sound which was inside it, and so really, the light of a thing and its song were just the same thing.

And there were days that the horse could see what she could hear, and hear what she could see. On those days, the silver and the feathers were happy indeed, because then everything was in just the right place.

But then sometimes, on other days, it was different, and then the weather would close in, and the idea of the maze would become something different altogether. It would become oppressive, and heavy. And then the wind and the rain and the sleet would come down, and it would bring a kind of darkness with it, and when these things came, the horse would shy, and she would tremble in the weather, and turn away from the darkness that had come down, and she would refuse to look.

And then her eyes, which were mostly so bright and clear, and had a sparkle of life in them, would grow downcast and hard, and she would paw at the ground, and be dissatisfied. She would be dissatisfied with everything, then.

One day, and then another. One after the other. Free and open, then downcast and hard.

*

There was only one entrance to Tritonis. It was a large gate, set into the wall which surrounded the city.

So tall was the gate that it was five times higher than the tallest horse on the island; taller even than the shadow made when the guardsman whose mount it was sat high on the great beast in his ceremonial armour with its feathers and fur all flying up around him and across his blue skin, so that he would look like a sunset — even this guardsman and his mighty horse were dwarfed in their height by the city gate.

No one in the city could remember a time, or had even heard of a time, when the gate had been closed, and the drawbridge across the moat drawn up. The moat had never been breached. This is no surprise, because it was so full of dark fears; things that crawled and slithered and stung, or things that were the dark shadows of themselves — but about these things and the moat and its awful depths we are not going to concern ourselves, because they are another story altogether, and one much more difficult than this.

In Tritonis lived many wonderful creatures, and other things besides. The city was large and sprawling, with many fantastic wonders, the dark things in the moat seemed an entire world away, and not just out of sight. It was not just the creatures who had lives, of course, but everything — because everything has habits, and everything with a habit is alive, of course.

So the buildings and the streets of Tritonis and all the

things in them had lives, because a life is precisely energy which comes in patterns and forms. But I hardly need to tell you that, of course.

*

In the city, among all the other habits and things, there lived a creature that looked like nothing so much as it looked like a serpent. In truth, even a casual glance could discern that it was not the typical type of snake that might steal your eggs or poultry, or digest a mouse in the sun, or have a water jug thrown at it as it escapes down a hole in the side of a stone water trough on a hot Sicilian day, or even slither away into the undergrowth at the approach of your footsteps. No, it wasn't that type of serpent at all, even though any of those are impressive enough in the way that they take hold of your attention and refuse to let it go. No, this serpent was the opposite; there was something about it that was hard to keep hold of, in your attention; so that it was inevitable that the city would see it, and then forget it, instantly, as though it had never existed at all, as though it was always a shadow, a set of circumstances that could change at any minute, or mean two things at once.

The serpent was a concomitant, an inevitable result, of the daily and ongoing life of the city. I know that I need to explain that. I will be brief.

No one or no thing deliberately created the serpent (the same could be said of everything, of course). But when you have a city the size of Tritonis, things are being created and uncreated all the time. And there can be remnants as things are formed, and there can be remnants as they fall apart, and since it is in the nature of things to aggregate in new ways even as they segregate from their old forms, and the overwhelming tendency of habits is to continue in some way, so it follows that from the remnants and pieces of things and habits new creatures arise, and so it was with the serpent. It was a serpent of pieces. A beast, full of serpentine habits, and made from many different things.

Its belly was covered with leather offcuts from the workshops of tailors and upholsterers, and its flanks and back were covered with the wall hangings that had been thrown out of the palace when the Empress had wanted a new colour scheme. For scales, the creature had pieces of armour cut from the blue bodies of slain soldiers, and to give some relief from the coldness of that, they were inlaid with patterns of dragons sporting in a sunset, created with shards of coloured glass taken from church windows and the kaleidoscopes of children long grown up.

The serpent's skeleton was made of the bones of every type of animal, of course, because to use anything else would just be fanciful...

For eyes, the serpent had two diamonds. Whether or not they were the real thing, I leave for you to decide, but if they were once the earrings of a railway workers' wife, you could hardly tell, so well were they cut. The serpent's fangs were the talons of a great kingfisher that had been caught and killed by an angry woman, and the venom that flowed through them was the bile of a creature that had been caught in a trap but never allowed to die, that had been made to suffer endlessly... such was the serpent, or at least its parts.

The buildings of the city among which the serpent would glide made and remade themselves continuously. In a way, they did this just like the trees and the creatures of the field where the horse ran and played; but there was something of a difference, and it was this: in the field outside the city, everything grew from within, so that its energy came from within it, even though the information still came from somewhere else; and in this way a tree or a beast seemed to grow from itself, even though there was so much going on around it.

But in Tritonis, nothing grew from inside itself. Not just the information, but also the energy, came from outside, from an act of energetic will from outside the creature or the thing. And this, really, was the difference between the city and the field, and it was a profound difference, that never ceased.

And the wall between the city and the field had therefore to be something profound in itself, for it had to keep the two apart, and that was why it was very high, and very thick, it was so as to keep the two apart. The wall was a special thing indeed, in the way it could glow like the sun, and leap with flame and light like the surface of the sun. It was as though to keep the city and the field separate was an act somehow like the sun itself.

The wall was a marvellous thing, because it allowed the city to forget that the moat was there. It could pretend that the moat was far, far away.

So, that should tell you everything you need to know about the wall and the gate, and the drawbridge, and the moat full of dark things. Which is passing strange, because those things are such an important part of this tale, and yet I am offering to tell you almost nothing about them. But you do have all the information you need, because the gate and the drawbridge were the way through the wall, and the way between the field and the city, and the way across the moat.

*

So the serpent lived in the depths of the city, among the houses and the public buildings and their shadows. At night it would slide along the roads, or down into the basements, or into the front doors and along the hallways and up the stairs and into the attics, and it would live there, in secret, keeping awake with all its coiling and uncoiling anyone foolhardy enough to try to sleep in the rooms below.

One day, it happened that the serpent had been asleep for five years in a particular room, the owners of which were long gone and forgotten. The serpent had spent all this time asleep on a pile of folded sheets and blankets that had never been used and were still in the monogrammed bags in which they had been brought home from the market on an autumn day, when it had seemed that it was getting colder and that some new warm blankets might be just the thing.

Nearby a table overflowed with diagrams and plans relating to a problem of mechanics and stars that in the end had become too complicated, and had been left unsolved by the owner. He had taken his family and gone off to a faraway country, where he took up painting and his wife took up music, the children taking up philosophy, architecture and medicine respectively, because all of those seemed, on the face of them, to be simpler.

And so the serpent had been asleep in this house for five years, undisturbed. And then one day, it was woken by a noise, a sound that could have been close, or far away, there was no telling. It seemed to be everywhere.

Further, it was impossible to tell if it was something opening or closing, or a kind of rolling thunder, or even, really, whether the sound involved movement at all. Such was the moment of confusion that the serpent experienced when it woke, hearing this sound.

And then there were footsteps, and the house was surely not used to *that*. To the house as well as the serpent they seemed especially unusual and peculiar, and the house felt its attention being held fast, and the serpent shared the feeling. And the serpent roused itself, and raised its head and looked, but there was nothing there to see in the gloom. Just the sound of hooves on the street outside.

Once it had begun, it happened every day.

Sometimes it felt as though a cool mist had come down on a day on which the sun was too fierce for comfort and the wind so hot that it burned; and the sound of the horse (for you know it was the horse, don't you...) moving in the streets of the city was the cool, relieving mist.

The day came that the serpent was out in the street, keeping to the walls and the shadows, as this had always been its habit, and the horse was there too, and finally the paths of the serpent and the horse crossed.

The serpent was for some reason heading out to the field, to help in some serpentine way in the construction of something, and the horse was for some equine reason heading into the city, for she had decided that to live always in the fields was simultaneously not enough and too much, and so the horse had decided that a house in the city was the thing, until the field felt like just the right thing. Because it was, of course, very important that everything feel like just the right thing.

And so somehow it was in a strange matter of housing that their paths crossed, and once it began one evening, they were straight away altogether crossed, and not just in their paths. Among the strings and feathers and wood and wire suddenly they knew the smell and the touch and the movement of each other, it was not just in their paths.

In the worlds of the horse and the serpent, everything became now very different. And the field and the city seemed to have somehow merged, as though the city walls were no longer there, and had somehow disappeared into the air.

Now, it is something universal that the first feeling anyone has when a wall disappears is a kind of elation, and an intoxication of freedom, and there is space, and a certainty that this is how things are meant to be, because the sense of space reaches into your blood, and it feels as though this is the first time that your blood is really flowing, as if it is moving across the space where the wall once was. It is like this for everyone. And this is how it was for both the horse and the serpent.

They became friends, and it was good for them both when they were together, even though they were so different, in shape and in everything. For what comparison, really, can there normally be between a serpent and a horse? Perhaps in very certain circumstances, between certain individuals, there might be a comparison. And so this must have been one of those circumstances. Somewhere, there was some basis for comparison.

And the serpent grew soon to feel somehow the same as the horse, and the serpent grew to love being near the horse, and soon there was a thing in each of them that was captivated by the other. The sounds that the serpent made would take the horse and hold her; and the way that the horse would move, and her voice, would take the serpent, and hold it, deep in its stillness, so that then it became like a rock, a small mountain made of rock.

For a time (and really, it was not a long time at all), the days went by in this fashion, and everything was fine. The serpent enjoyed to his rock-like, reptilian depths the captivating musk scent of the horse, and the horse, for her part, enjoyed the sounds that the serpent made as it slid and clanked from one street or one building or one chord of shadow to another, she enjoyed it all, in herself.

And they both enjoyed the touch of each other, the feeling of each other, and that touch, and the feeling of it, was at the core of them, at the core of the thing that they created between them.

It may have been strange, for a serpent and a horse, but it was a thing that was between them.

*

Time passed, and the weather became variable. It varied more and more, from day to day. There might be sunshine among the trees one day, then dry, violent crackling clouds among the higher reaches of the buildings along the streets of the city the next, followed by a spell of dark mist rolling off the moat, off its still, deep blackness. And then there might be a day or two of rain, which would wash everything clean and wash away the weather, so that everything could start again — but it was always only so that there could be more weather, and it could start all over again.

One day there was a crack of lightning and a great, heavy, peal of thunder came falling down out of the sky like something liquid and heavy. Together the lightning, like an angry youth, and the thunder, like a great winged horse with rolling hooves, disturbed everything, and together showed a tusked, hard face to everything.

What had been just the weather of the day now became the weather of everything. And then it became the world itself; and when it was dark, or light, or warm, or cold in the sky above the city and across the field, it was dark or light or warm or cold even in the hearts of the serpent and the horse, as though the weather had somehow come from outside them and into them. They had made themselves open to it, and now it was inside them.

And then an ice would form over their hearts, and something in them was lost. And sometimes it would eventually thaw from inside itself, or other times the sun would beat down on them, so that even as the ice was thawing, they would feel themselves turning to dust, drying up inside because of the heat of the sun. The weather had ceased altogether to be their friend, and had become something else.

The ice grew thicker and stronger between them, forcing them apart. And as the distance between them grew, and the things that had seemed good to them began to evaporate and disappear almost as if they had been only phantoms all along — as this happened, they actually felt more truly in the picture. More truly, as though they were in the real world now, and no longer in the one on which they had spent so much effort, on trying to keep everything from unravelling.

It was as if all that had been somehow unreal, and now they were clearly in the picture. Their falling apart had become inevitable, as inevitable as the day and the night. This was the real picture.

But they each still had their own views. Increasingly, the serpent found that it could do nothing right. When there was somehow any noise, it was sure to be wrong somehow, and the horse would rear, and become ill-tempered. Her temper was becoming short — nothing was good enough, or short enough, or long enough, or high enough, or went on for long enough. Nothing was enough.

And sometimes the serpent would be stirred by this, and

the feeling was new to it, for in truth many feelings were new to it, constructed as it was, and when something went wrong the serpent would stir and raise its head to strike, as if there was an instinct in its venom. But it would not strike, for it was afraid of something in the ice that it could feel gathering between them. The uncoiling, the unravelling that it could feel between them.

The horse grew more and more unhappy, and soon refused to have anything to do with the serpent. The serpent would reach to touch the horse, and the horse would shudder in some anger, and move away, and refuse to look or talk. Sometimes the horse would look down at the ground with dark, angry eyes, and she would retreat to the field, to wander alone among the trees, and then it would seem to the horse that nothing had changed at all.

And the drawbridge across the moat would be raised. At first the other creatures of the city thought that this was unusual, but it happened more and more often; the drawbridge would be raised, so that nothing could pass, and the serpent would be left alone under the shadows of the raised bridge, unable to lower it, and at this the serpent became confused, for it could do nothing. The mechanism of the drawbridge was an inviolable mystery, sealed as if there was no way on earth to influence it or understand it.

And each time the drawbridge raised, and removed the field and the city from each other, it would stay raised for longer than the time before. Always longer, and this was a mystery too. And the little horse would walk among the trees of the field and she would look at them with her dark, angry eyes, and sometimes she would imagine everything black, and dead, and gone.

And there was something else there along with that

blackness and the hard emptiness that the horse felt behind her dark eyes. It was something heavy, and black, and it was conscious, and it would laugh in a hard kind of way when it was seeing through her eyes. A hard kind of strength, sure of its victory. And it reached out in its blackness and its strength, and it began to strangle the serpent. The serpent could not breath. It writhed, trying to free itself, but the grip around its throat was like bands of steel, and the strength of it was unstoppable.

The thing that was dark and conscious laughed at the weakness of the serpent, and how it struggled to no avail, how it flailed and writhed to no avail. And when it could see that the serpent had given up, and ceased in its struggling, and was waiting to die, it released its grip and laughed and taunted and was gone, and the serpent gasped, and breathed as if the breath were its first, after an eternity.

And now all of the world to the horse seemed to be full of nothing but hateful, petty creatures, and although she feared the outcome, to the horse it seemed as though the serpent had become one of those; a hateful, petty creature, who, the shadow inside her said, deserved really nothing more than to be hated, but at a safe distance, because hate is so contagious.

And to the serpent, the world had become full of vengeful, irascible creatures that could only judge, and most harshly, and so it seemed that they in turn must be judged just as harshly. And soon the horse came in the serpent's eyes to be one of these harsh, irascible creatures, and to deserve, at any distance, the same treatment, to be judged for its judgement.

So soon, everything was hateful, and harsh, and judged. And so everything began to separate, and to close down, and soon there was nothing.

And now the drawbridge was raised and did not come down. Everything was separate. In the moat the things that lived there stirred, as if the water was filled with blood, and there was something big, that was like the shadow of the serpent and also like the shadow of the horse, that heaved in chaos and rode the bottom of the moat, down into the earth, darkly.

And the horse and the serpent could not talk any more, because of a weight pressing down on their hearts. They would try, and they tried and tried, but it was always as though there was nothing that could be done.

Everything defeated them now.

Everything was raw, and bloody, but now the horse and the serpent realised that what they had really wanted, all along, was something different. What they had been seeking was not in their small hearts. All along it had been in the heart that does not change, that never tires under the weight of any load that it bears. The bigger heart, that is strong and tireless.

And now it was clear, how they had come together, and then come apart, as they travelled across the curved surface of the torus of everything, each in their spiral paths, across the surface of the torus. Their paths had brought them together for a while, and they had moved in a kind of dance for a while, in a proximity to each other, both wanting to unite, but not between them being capable of it. Their paths had not really united, ever, and so they had to grow apart, and in this they had no choice, because movement is movement, and a torus is a torus.

As they moved along their paths, across the expanding surface of the torus, near the apogee of its possibilities, they had moved apart, and they kept moving apart, and it was not easy, for the connection between the spirit of the horse and the spirit of the serpent had become deep, even though it was now shot through with a bitterness. And so they moved apart, in a long, drawn-out dance of distance and estrangement.

And there was a sadness everywhere and an emptiness, and in it, what joy there had been for them floated away like smoke. The torus had moved on, and was supporting other things; it was not supporting them any more.

*

Eventually the land was destroyed. It became waste, and barren, because when they fought, the land and the water and the air all retreated in horror, and it was hard to breathe; everything seemed to gasp for breath. And finally nothing could live there any more, not even the horse and the serpent, for they could not breathe any more; they had to gasp for air, and even the water turned to bile in their blood now.

*

But the universe is not cruel, nor is it heartless. It saw how hard the horse and the serpent were trying; and how hopeless and caught up they were, caught up in things and each other, so that nothing worked, and the harder they tried, the harder everything became, all caught up, and not working.

And so the universe sent the spirit of the kingfisher, and it flew across the land where the horse and the serpent now fought ceaselessly. As the kingfisher flew, three feathers from its tail fell to the ground.

The first feather fell down and was weighed against the land, and the idea of the land was heavier than the feather, and so the feather was happy to become the fields and the plains and the mountains; and so it became the land.

The second feather fell down and was weighed against the water, and the water was heavier than the feather, and so the feather was content to become part of the rivers and the streams and lakes and the rain that fell down from the sky; and so the second feather became the water.

And the third feather was weighed against the sky, but even the air was heavier than the feather, and the feather was overcome in joy by a large cumulus, and it disappeared, and so the feather became part of the wind and the clouds and the air, and all the things that move in the air.

And because all three feathers were weighed against a thing that was heavier than themselves, the land and water and air all came to exist in a new way. This was the gift of the kingfisher in this, and it was a necessary gift, because the land and everything on it had become poisonous, and waste.

And so everything that been held in place for any reason at all now fell away, and everything broke apart.

*

And in this way the horse soon regained her freedom, and one day woke to find that she had gained a pair of wings, which she could use to fly above the storms, so that they no longer frightened her, and soon she had control of the skies and the storms, and the sound of her hooves across the sky was a welcome sign.

And as for the serpent, it slowly gained wisdom, which is no mean feat, even for a serpent.

And neither of them were afterwards ever the same again, the horse who could fly wherever she chose, and the serpent who had learned much, and neither of them saw things in the same way ever again.

From that time onwards, horses and serpents did not have

anything to do with each other; they lived in different worlds, and it was better that way. Above the storms, and above not knowing, respectively.

*

Thousands of lifetimes passed, and many ages later, the bones of a horse and a serpent were unearthed.

On one end of the island of Mene, where there had once been the great city of Tritonis, the workers found the bones and teeth and scales of a serpent. At the other end of the island, where there had once been a great field of trees and open spaces, they found the bones of a horse, and the horse, it turned out, was not so little after all. These were the remains of great creatures, not small or slight ones.

But now here is the thing, and it was really at the core of the report that the workers made to the investigators who were sent. You see, the heart of the horse was not there, it was never found; and the heart of the serpent was not there, and so it was never found either. Where the hearts had gone was a great mystery to the investigators, who fidgeted with their hats, and were confused and went home.

And it was only then, after the investigators had left, that the workers found in the earth the remains of the great drawbridge which had been the gateway into Tritonis. And beside the remains they found, perfectly preserved, the body of a kingfisher, .

The last time anyone had seen it, the last time it had been mentioned in the history, the drawbridge had been raised, and nailed shut with spikes as long as the stings that had tormented Io as she wandered. But now the drawbridge was collapsing and disintegrating, and the earth was reclaiming it, and it was impossible to tell any more whether it was raised or lowered, or somewhere in between.

The workers wondered at this, and then they wondered at how a kingfisher could have come to be here, but they didn't wonder for long, and soon they gave up, and went home.

The field of trees was gone, and nowhere to be seen, and the city was gone, and nowhere to be seen, and that was neither right nor wrong. And somewhere beyond that, there was another field of green grass, and the world was too full to talk about.

POEMS

THE HOUND OF EMPEDOCLES

The hound of Empedocles lies deep in slumber;
his dreams are hot and of Nickneven,
and other awful Scottish hags.

Nidhogg the serpent gnaws
at the root of the ash
and all the while,
unconcerned that this may fall,

Empedocles in his purple robe
regards the breeze that scours the clouds
that through the day obscured the view –

the airships of the Northern King;
battlefields that sing and sprawl
on black and golden sand
where the Emperor did ordain;
he raised his hand
and so our mighty yet ungainly
Hephaestus made so thus:

Prometheus lies in chains,
surrounded by his precious, senseless, clock.

Prometheus, laid low, in the broken wreck
of the ship that once did rule the sky;
was in turn the flagship of the Emperor's fleet —
the mighty Roc that crashed and burned...

The hound that slumbers on
lives in Copenhagen and the Port as one —
one bronze sandal chewed in each,
depending on which eye is open;

on which hand the deity that dances raises
as the sky beneath its feet unravels to a pulse
and in that pulse does play that tune of separate notes
that bind all Copenhagen and the Port as one
to the wheel that turns in concert with the sun
that rises on Copenhagen and the Port as one;

This rain persisted until it filled the world,
the seven boroughs of the town are islands now;

water lies between them dark and deep
and full of things which of dark deep violence speak;
and all the streets are gone,
and all the air is dark;
the baker and his wife
sit surrounded by their sourdough
and that sputtering flame that flecks
the dark face of all the world with a little light,
and all is lost...

in Copenhagen, they have deconstructed toast...

The hound of Empedocles lies deep in slumber.
His dreams are hot, and of Nickneven
and all those awful Scottish hags.

Nidhogg the serpent gnaws.
Such is the root of the ash.

*

TRAVEL TO ALLAHABAD

How shall we mark this dry bed?
The river Saraswati no longer flows in this world;
pale shadows alone are cast upon this bed —

From the Himalayas to the sea,
the Saraswati led, wide and deep,
clear in the light of the world;

twelve cities ranged along its length;
life just as we know it
drew upon those waters wide and deep,

and now, how shall we know its dry bed?

All the words and all the music in the world
flowed in the waters of this world and the next,
between the world of formless things,
and their shadows that we know
as cast upon the world,
as things of bone, and iron, and stone;
which once spoke for themselves to hearing
which now dries and bleaches in the sun;

all twelve cities have gone beneath the sand,
and now the Saraswati flows in the formless world alone,
invisible to mortal eyes —

now, how shall we know this dry bed?

To see the Saraswati, travel to Allahabad,
to the confluence of the three great rivers,
and there, for those with wisdom,
Saraswati will make herself visible.

ALL 1,000 SONGS

1.

Ali ibn Nafi Ziryab has memorised
all one thousand songs from beginning to end.

He has added a fifth string to his lute;
he has taken to using eagle's talons to pluck the strings.
Without his music, Beauty would be mute;
the Jinn would have nothing to sing.

The Jinn teach Ziryab music every night.
When thus awakened, he calls for his friends;

his slaves Ghazzalan and Hinda rise
and take up their lutes, and the three
pass the night deep in talk, with music, and sighs,
after which they retire to sleep.

In this manner, Ali ibn Nafi Ziryab has memorised
all one thousand songs from beginning to end.

He is proud of his agility; he writes and sings
of nomads and vagabonds, and death and desire.
If there is an end to his ability
it lies beyond his descriptions of deserts and his satire.

In this manner, Ziryab has entertained and surprised
all of society; of his fame and wealth there is no end.

2.

A Princess arrives,
she bears ultimata from her father in the North.
A train of camels bears her, their faces turned to the sea.
Ziryab and she will talk as they walk forth
upon the shining surface of the sea.

A gift of Isis — a waxing moon — rises
and of the surface and the beauty of the sea,
there is no end.

The moon embraces the mouth of the water,
and the mountains and the valleys bend —
where Ziryab and the Princess lay their feet
upon the water,
it floods with light without an end or centre.
In the Princess from the North, Isis has her daughter.

Delicious were those days they spent together
while Fate slept!

She binds him in chains
more firmly every second he beholds her.
The universe folds upon itself;
the earth is echoed in the sky,
she is reflected in the stars;
the plants and animals alone know the secret of her.

This magic is not some cheap box
of courtesan tricks or weighted die,
nor some religious manual
on how to suffer or to die;

and when her work of state is done and ends,
she is gone before the morning light descends
and as she leaves, her father's army descends,
and the Caliphate in al-Andalus ends...

Fire spreads and feeds on blood
and beds are steeped in blood
and in their beds are killed for love
all the friends that Ziryab thought to love
and the soldiers of the Northern King
do not spare a single thing;

Ziryab climbs the hill beyond his city,
and alone with the plants and animals, he cries:

'What have you done?
What have you done?
Is there no pity?'

The world does not reply.

3.

Now Ziryab is false gold that does not survive the assize.
The gold-tester is no friend of his; he throws Ziryab aside;

Ziryab stands before the sunrise,
shattered into pieces,
and he is content to die,
for love may enter lightly,
but its end is serious,
and now he is bound in chains,
and is content to die.

From the silence of the ground,
Isis roars at the rising sun; at the sound
Ali ibn Nafi Ziryab unfolds and falls to the ground.

The cripple's stick becomes a sword,
the gazelle, trembling,
a lion that roars and eats the world;
but today a heart is all that will be carved.

The heart of Ziryab has taken many forms;

a field for a grazing beast,
a jungle for a hunting one,
a temple for an idol,
a book for a scholar,
a bed for a lover;
but now it takes just one...

Ali ibn Nafi Ziryab and the Princess of the North
will meet by tunnelling,
as mines in the same ground wordless meet —
for carrier pigeons lose their way and forget all sound,
as the sky shifts beneath their worded feet —

As for unrequited, refined love — let others have it!

'Give me contentment,' Ziryab says.
'Kiss me, embrace me, give me the rest...
I am dead to the world, just give me this...!'

In this manner, Ali ibn Nafi Ziryab has forgotten
all one thousand songs from beginning to end.

*

THE UNSPEAKABLE KANGAROO

Among the rocks,
Helen sprang to her feet
and swiftly, lithely fled.

The sun was still high then;
it was a hard blue white,
it was cold, it burned the sky.
Ice burns like that, from the inside out;

He had said to her:
"Helen! Do you not wonder about the sun?
Yellow, was it not, once?"
Helen did not want to speak of this,
and they fought.

"At least, Helen," he said,
"spend the night in the car, don't go far.
Spend the night listening to something
reassuring — Schubert,
or grounding, like Bach.

"Do not listen to Shostakovitch —
for Shostakovitch was not known
for doing favours,
and he is not going to start with you."

The night from which the kangaroo emerged was black.
It had settled hard, like black ice on a road.

The kangaroo was six feet or more tall,
if he existed at all;
as solid as one of those Egyptian statues he was,
the way they seem to stand on the edge of everything;
in the silence he waited and did not move.

His eyes overflowed with darkness
and did not move;

Simon approached the kangaroo
where it stood and did not move;
he reached up and laid a hand upon its face.

You could ask a mountain to hear you;
or just as well this apparition
that if it were to move
would split the ground
in two without a sound
and of the witness leave no trace.

Something like Horus on a rooftop,
and he has bought infinity to the dawn,
and you are something to do with Seth, perhaps,
some lackey of mortality, the end of it all...
flee the light, for Horus is on the rooftop —

Helen arrived at dawn with the sun on her back,
back at the point from which she had fled;
music they did not discuss.

A veil had drawn behind her;
she held a book,
and she had drawn pictures, of kangaroos,
in the spaces on the pages of this book
that he had never seen before;

(it was in fact the manual,
taken from the document pocket
of the Falcon's farside door).

Now the circumference may be small enough,
but the axle moves to a baritone,
and when the Falcon starts, its engine roars to life;

Horus leaves the roof,
and flies into the sunrise,
the golden spokes of which form chords, suspended,
that never will resolve to a tonic or to proof,

and the Falcon no longer sits upon the roof
with its gaze upon the silence
in which the kangaroo does wait
with darkness in its eyes
and does not move.

*

MACHINIST TIPPIT

To us, high in our library,
once a week there came,
in his steaming, clanking, leviathanic walker,
the Cardinal's man,
a Machinist, by rank, named Tippit.

He was so well suited,
in his hermetically capable well-stitched leather,
eyeshieldings of obsidian glass,
air filters of hydrolised heather,
accoutremented with dark silk and brass,
that you could not tell him —
without close inspection —
from one of his Lords, on a good day,
or one of his villeins, on most.

Behind his mask,
behind his suit, above his boots,
we never saw his look, his face;
he was — then — just another Cardinal's man.

His head bowed most courteous to Hypatia
and he would never enter further than the foyer,
but still — you could hear his god in his voice
and at his side always, his weapon,
buckled in, true, holstered appropriately,
but we were all agreed —
we could see his god creeping there, as well.

Perhaps to Machinist Tippit
as his steam-powered walker-bolo cross
thundered through the night
we were not much more, even then, than lepers or lint;
but — no, that can't be right…

For with his studied reserve and deliberate disdain,
he made such pointed and apparent effort
despite himself, that it was plain

we meant something to the man…
When he arrived on Thursdays
with his officially sanctioned,
confirmed-in-triplicate load,
Hypatia would bring him,
wonderfully crafted,
exquisitely calligraphed,
correct in every detail
(aesthetic as well as technical),
a hand-written consignment note
which Machinist Tippit never failed
to impale, pointedly, on a spike,
without reading what she wrote.

The message was clear.

His vehicle was large.
It clanked. There was steam, and smoke.
His armour hard and resolute,
his raiment airtight and functional;
the new air would never get to him —

but as to the man's inner nature,
the attitude of his soul,
the heft of his philosophy,
it probably serves us best
to return to where we began:

Machinist Tippit,
masked, armoured, hermetically sealed,
was, beyond all doubt,
and to the end,
the Cardinal's man.

*

MYSTERY AND MELANCHOLY

The Sun shines from the right
on a Girl transfigured by the Sun to Shadow.
Running into a Shadow darker than Night,
she pushes a hoop with a stick.

Behind the Girl transfigured by the Sun to Shadow
her hair flows Behind Her as
she pushes the hoop with a stick
toward the setting Sun Before Her.

Her hair flows Behind Her as
a shadow moves in from the right
(toward the setting Sun Before Her).
The Shadow of the building on the right
is darker than the night.

The Shadow moves in from the Right.
Beneath a flag that flies above it
the Shadow of the building on the right
is darker than the night.
Behind it, a Wagon waits with Open Doors.

Beneath the flag,
a Long Building glows white in the Setting Sun.
In the shade the Wagon waits with Open Doors,
towards which the Girl with the Hoop Runs.

She is frozen in mid-stride,
running into that Shadow Darker than the Night.
The Long Building has many small windows,
upon which the Sun shines from the right.

*

ONE FALCON WING

One falcon wing of many feathers
hides a winding road,
most perfect in elevation and perspective!
Such counterweights, three hundred feet tall,
are in place across the Lower Kingdom.

All belong to me, the Osiran;
the daily commerce, life,
the parade of love —
at the first step of the stairway to heaven,
my elbows are supported by two attendants.

The walls are distressed,
and could give way at any moment.
There is nothing but me to stop you from falling,
for all belongs to me.

I have a crook in the market, in the shadows.
If he is to be believed,
the Upper Kingdom has a long arm.

As for the tower,
this mountain of rooms and bricks —
as if by a white shroud,
its peak is obscured by clouds,
and a single falcon wing.

*

I DISPATCHED A FLIGHT
OF HORNETS

I dispatched a flight of hornets earlier today.
I signed the paper myself with dark ink;
on the back of some rustling, unreadable paper;
something tedious, to do with the end of history...

On the back of it,
one thousand yellowjackets I ordered deployed
to the theatre south of the front at Oster Hornum;
a wonderful military advance, these, my hornets,
a most clever union; the genes of a giant squid,
an English oak, a llama and a pumpkin,
with a dormouse thrown in, slavering at the bit —
all combined in *vespa mandarinia*
in a delicate composition of earth and dust
that could have fallen from the lips
of the colossi, King and Queen, of Memnon...

when the King and Queen of Memnon still sang, that is,
before the frost came and cracked their hips,
took out their eyes, and sealed their lips...

From there my hornets flew to where
the offending star in the evening gloom
sparkled like a light inside a room;
and that could not be mistaken;

My hornets found the trail,
through twisted gorse and bracken
undergone most terminal travail;
that molten glow of burnished bronze
was not to be mistaken
for a beast with breath,
or water caught upon the sun;
and there were found, in all,
sheltered by a broken wall,
two creatures, mechanical,
all surprised and overcome.

Neither threat nor argument was had,
every tendency to winding down
was fed and given its head;
a singular event, overflowing,
not about to be repeated...

One of these automatons:
a walrus made with otter's feet for flight
with splines of Newton's theory and facts
and many multi-coloured fins with which
to cut the air all around into slices thin
its bulk and slide in silence
through counterveils of glimmer and of light;

The other creature:
made to wind between
the dark and muffled depths of northern fjords and bays
upon the aspect of which the mechanical gaze
of these unknowing machines once rested;
this dark contusion of error now is tested:

This machinery insists
that what cannot be seen
is not *per se* at odds with —
and can be in between —
all that which upon the world
is there absolutely,
necessarily, to be seen —

and this same machinery, I am told,
insists upon the silence of the wind
and the air that hovers
in the strings of harps which now are mute
and in which so much slumbers — unrealised, they say...
this, the awful rationality of their numbers...

The tendency of clockwork,
in these dark and muffled depths,
where nothing can be seen,
and which of course the Empire in its wisdom
so thoroughly rejects,
is to turn in wonder to the clarity
of wind that whispers perfect numbers
(so they say) and cries in joy for measurements
that have and number
a beginning, a middle, and an end.
They do not require belief —
and they scorn our every free-of-place
and dogvillesque attempt
to deconstruct the meaning
of the metal pegs of tents;
and they say that we attempt
to reduce these things to a fiction
of irrational and non-existent numbers,

and endless strings of quantum almost-blunders...
and that we then donate the lot to charity,
since it has no value in or of itself...

(*Of course, it is more complex than that;*
no wonder they can't understand it;
the value of a thing, most clearly,
is that it can be dissected...)

So, satisfied now as to the acquiescence
of these two specimens so artfully detained,
by hornets that were so well and academically trained,
so I, Leopold von Chow,
Captain of the Carapaced Horse, First Class,
decorated of course,
do present as a personal gift,
both of these former belligerents

(*as mentioned above,*
once most lethally dangerous,
now as gentle as chloroformed doves)

to Facilitator, Mediator, Literary Theoretician,
Professor of Biology and the new Liturgical Repetition,
The Most Good Doctor, State Minister,
Advocate for the Quantum Bypass,
Professor Hans Dovrefjell-Hass...

Sir,
these creatures are committed to you as gifts.
May only good things come to pass.

*

TWELVE BOATS

Twelve boats in a circle,
all pointing towards the centre.

On each one so much went on
but the crews are gone,
everything is dropped,
the decks are empty.

Twelve boats are empty, in a circle,
all pointing towards the centre.

The coast is not visible,
there is no wind,
the cargo is intact.
There is no wind to raise the waves.

There is no wind to raise the waves
and the sea is glass.

Below, bones are washed clean.

*

THE PARTY

1.

Some swore that the party had been planned forever;
others opined it to be a spur of the moment affair.

Regardless of the intentions or their genesis, in the end
five were invited; the evening was set to be pleasant!

but fat, greedy Sight crashed the party —
and so it turned out that the usual six,
the same old gang, were there...

2.

There was plenty of fresh meat there,
and drink, laid out on tables that went on forever.

The evening could have been quite pleasant;
the place was soon up to its neck
in the chatter that comes with a party —

Hearing had no idea where or when *that* would end;
so many inflections and subtleties

— double entendres everywhere!

— what an affair!

3.

As for Sight, what he sees, you see, he yells;
it's never a quiet affair.
Sight cleared the table in five minutes flat;
he ate everything there!
Boorish Sight, of his crassness and appetite,
there is no end!

Touch and Hearing sat in the corner on the deco couch;
this was just another loud party!

Taste and Smell would rather be elsewhere, that was clear;
these things go on forever...

Memory just hoped that the evening could be salvaged,
and somehow turn out to be, well... pleasant.

4.

But what Memory might recall as pleasant
is rarely what actually happens;

here at this party, sly, wanton Touch
had his own idea of a good time,
and Touch felt, as the others all knew,
that Sight, if he could, would eat forever,
until there was nothing left to see;

and so while Sight was not looking,
while Sight's gaze was turned from there,
Touch and the others hatched a plan:

Sight's antisocial nonsense would come at last
to a most deserved end!

5.

A first edition of Decartes was found in the study,
covered in disfiguring graffiti from beginning to end;

Memory drew a blank;
had no idea what was going on there.

Smell was about to confess to the affair,
his defence being the intolerable stench of dualism,
when someone leaned against the light switch;
the consequent darkness was straightaway most pleasant!

They all, save Sight, wished to themselves
that this reprieve could last forever;
for Apollo having quit the room,
it was now the mere shadow of a party.

6.

Sight, the naughty insatiable thing,
fled the party in a most upset state,
thinking that he would be this hungry forever!

With that departure, at last,
the febrile, awkward scene came to an end.

Smell was on the balcony, breathing in the Moon,
arm in arm with Memory, who got there
not a moment too soon, but forgot why,
and Touch and Taste were in neotenic bliss
in the hot tub, starting an affair;

Hearing just enjoyed the silence of not being seen.

The evening had slowed down like a big fat Buddha,
upon whose expanse they all played unseen,
and it was, therefore, exceptionally pleasant.

7.

Every day they throw the same party,
it never really ends.

Sight always comes back the next morning,
promising to behave. He will do that forever;

So they live in the hope,
the rest of them there,
that if he will just evolve,
life might become what they've read,
and heard, and feel it can be —

an affair at once exceptionally pleasant,
refined, yet not constrained, and
requiring no undue amount of care.

*

THE GREAT ROC

The city had been deserted by the Caliphate.

The army of the Northern King
placed plaques and notices
and around these within hours
numberless, limitless flocks of parrots gathered.

In the beak of each was
the manifesto of a new fresh religion,
bakey crusty fresh,
one that millions of swallows
would be able to cohere to
without dropping a wing or a heartbeat;
not one of them would question anything

(just as Adam's skull,
in its niche in the cathedral,
never questioned anything);

The parrots in a mass
would fly into the cathedral
so that from there
the shameful liar bird
would take fright,
and run from the building,
flightless, screaming the meaning
of the plaques and notices.

A singing pheonix would chase it close behind,
and together they would leap
into a burning bush in the centre of town.

The cathedral collapsed one day.

A crowd gathered, chewing on medlar and parrot.
The bishop of the cathedral
strove to wake them from their slumber
in caves without fish
where the water is clear and still...

Now the liar bird knows nothing of all this —
it desires nothing but your lovely pink mouth —
it is surreptitious,
unspeakable,
it is a gaudy peacock.

The parrots are teaching themselves to read
the plaques and notices, but
there is something already old
about parrots
in rockets that will not launch
on a journey into space,
into the eye of the great Roc,
as it turns around inside its skin
so that you, eventually,
are out of sight.

*

THE SCYTHIAN HORSE ARCHER

The horse looks set to soar into the sky;
it rears as if the blood that sustains its flesh
is tireless.

The tail sweeps back, carried by the charge
of the Scythian horse archer.

To the south the classical world shakes
beneath the horse's wordless feet,
and the Asian steppes are vast.

Fires burn in the night.
A field of stars.

*

THE FUNDAMENTAL QUESTION

There is a bird missing.
There are two in place.

One sees to its nest, attending,
the second has lit upon a branch, and sits,
but the third is missing.

The ground from where the bird was taken
bears tear marks where the bird is missing.

It is not possible to see the horse in its entire state.

In front of it is a building, the windows of which
are filled with black. It is impossible to see;
but it is obvious and clear that the horse is in pieces.

The pieces of horse are surrounded by red.
To get anywhere, you have to go past the horse
in pieces, surrounded by red —
the horse is nowhere to be seen;
the pieces of its flesh are blue and grey.

I can see this with what clarity I can
because of a broken window
that appears to be no accident.

*

THE MONUMENTAL LIE

This talk of stone and cutting stone implies
that the Revolution's Monument be built, but
irrationality in numbers is a monumental lie...

The Peoples' Provisional Council decries
any attempt to stifle or kill
what this talk of stone and cutting stone implies;

A contract is signed, the price insanely high —
for one thousand tons of marble and granite!
(Irrationality in numbers is a monumental lie...)

It takes ten thousand workers a good part of their lives
to shape the rock so as to iterate
what this talk of stone and cutting stone implies;

The Council have debated at least a dozen times
which Quantum Truth to Commemorate, but
irrationality in numbers is a monumental lie...

In the end a Committee won the Design Prize
and for a statue of Truth we are still waiting —
for as this talk of stone and cutting stone implies,
irrationality in numbers is a monumental lie.

*

GORGON

In stone, broken
edges glow in the light from the window.
Daughter of Phorcys and Ceto,
long steeped in the sands of Africa:

as you slept, endless centuries
gathered about you,
and now Osiris is begging alms,
throneless, at the gates of day.

*

STATIC

In the corner
stand three guns;
two new twenty twos
and a 303
stolen from the army.

Above them,
a CB radio
that stays on channel four
grizzles static
and occasionally voices.

*

TANIWHA

You move among the endless rows
of machines that shred and card wool;
from bale to hopper it goes,
and finishes wound upon a spool.

The noise is huge and deafening,
the only times it stops
are tea, and half-hour lunchtimes,
and when the yarn breaks, or drops.

The Maori priestess runs the shed.
You're sure she knows the inner working
of every cog and gear that screams
for wool, above a stream of silence
in which even the most casual of your glances
makes out the taniwha, lurking.

*

8:55

Time shudders at seven a.m.

The first cruel shake,
then the rush to the bell,
preceded by three minutes
of impossibly thin, inane, music.

If time would pause, then I would
use the resulting safe house of a moment
to remove every convoluted hypotactic door
from its hinges
and turn it into a wonderful unarrangement
of parataxis, unreferred, self-evident;

Where the uncorresponding inner life
of each school lunch, uniform,
lost shoe, fought-over hair tie, half full, half drunk,
glass of over-sugared chocolate and grumbling
at the world and you,
the piercing purple plastic flute,
and the ticking countdown to 8.55 —

are all unencumbered, set adrift and free,
answerable only to themselves
each event its own untrammelled Aristotlean
entelechy set free,
hypotaxia undone, unravelled —

Do I ask too much?

The immediate result is this:

every injured limb is treated
with magic eyevaydic honey
and magic eyevaydic gauze;

and that the small one is a spell
is easily remembered,
for the moon he does shine full
upon the still surface
of that paused, unrushed moment,
where even the huntsman under the chair
is content to stay for the moment, just there...

and remembering,
turn off every creaking electric light,
then time rebooted,
emerge, unblinking, into the sunlight.

And the sun rises in a meditating cat
holding court on a patch of warm porch
and no less, it shines
in the heart of the single moment now,
that reaches, changeless, from 7 a.m. to 8:55.

And in that sunlight,
everything catches fire anew,
and above it all,
a kookaburra, this time, watches dragonflies,
as they draw flame anew.

It is 8.55, and we are not late.

*

FINDING THE WEIGHT
OF THE MOON

Finding the weight of the moon —
a ludicrous proposition,
and it clamours for consideration...
there is a choice of boots
for feet that walk the maze
beneath the ground on which
the keep and moat are raised;

In the nesting chamber
rests the dark of the moon.
Death's own moon skin is broken
and all the words fly around his head
like little moons.

The child is upside down.
Death has a lotus beside each foot,
and from the dark of the moon,
the dogs with smiling faces turn,
and Death he smiles, he will wait his turn.

It is a ludicrous proposition this,
this finding the weight of the moon,
beneath the ground, where all the words
are like little moons.

*

7:49 (TRAIN)

She has a magical smile.
It's not meant for him,
but he intercepts the odd one
like a sneak thief.

When she laughs,
there is a tilt of the head
that is quite intoxicating.
She doesn't know that she does it.

Sometimes, he works for these;
sometimes, it's just a matter of waiting —
either way, they always come.
Then, he is happy.

*

THIS IS PORT DOG

This is Port Dog;
as unlikely a slum as ever spread
on the shores of a sea;
this sea, this sprawl in space,
this tangle of demented souls;
from what bell here
did ears shrink in dread?

This is Port Dog; for those entangled,
it is but one door removed from Hell.

Over the years, the wealth in the place
has slid from the hills,
slunk down to the docks —
it was most naturally money that led
the way to the shores of the sea,
where the sprawling space
is filled to the brim like a golden carapace
and here the darkest water laps;
here gold turns back into lead.

This is Port Dog;
it is unquestionable — what other place
could be so perfect an address for
Wyfurge, Tale, and Hammer (Mrs) —
where the shops and the docks
and the whores and the voyeurs
carouse by the shore of the sea,
and every embrace causes a ledger
in the rooms of Wyfurge, Tale, and Hammer (Mrs)

to quiver in doubt-free, remorseless anticipation
of deep, unending, and depending on specifics,
multiple, profit...

Port Dog sprawls and lies,
addled in luxury, unconscious, insensate,
among the leaden trinkets it makes from gold
that is transported ship by ship crate after crate
from markets new and old.

You may know Port Dog, perhaps;
but the only place that you can buy
a map to show you where and why
the Port is hidden from general view
is the Port itself, of course, and why?

The only true citizens
of this place that roars and glitters,
that has never really settled
into its skin near the edge
of the implacable sea —

the true citizens of this remorseless place
that hides from general view —
the real wastes of space —

are Zeus, that royal fuckup,
and that despicable, risible,
loathsome little toad, Mercury;
not you.

*

WYFURGE'S LETTER

Mrs Hammer, the Empire's lawyer,
works beside a mirror
before which a single candle
in dark walnut burns through the night.

Several doors along the corridor,
Colonel Tale (ret.) snores, feet up among
piled depositions, which
with exacting recourse to existing law
inkily outline the case
against this Provisional Editor,
this Bacon,
by whom Port Dog has been so very much disturbed,
and who by now can surely be no longer
so entirely, resolutely sure that he is in the right,
or so Colonel Tale, retired, has read,
to his inestimable satisfaction.

For three weeks and maybe more,
Mister Wyfurge has been away,
undercover at the docks,
shirtsleeved in dust and sweat,
seeking evidence admissible
of interlocutions, both casual and noteworthy,
and damage done by rumours mongered in the town;
of how words could be responsible
(what rare plucked fruit is that!)
for this pausing in the rate
at which the waters were by all measures going down...

all this nonsense; talk of ways to set the world to rights,
all this nonsense and ostenta,
when there is real work to be done,
both day and night!
Not *this* nonsense. And now some insist
that the water is rising at night...

Yes, the water is rising at night.

Wyfurge's report has appeared under the door;
a comprehensive, detailed account
in almost indecipherable scrawl
— a spider's web upon the sea —
delivered by a hand
hired by Mister Wyfurge for the price
of a warm and short-lived candle
to hold against the darkness of the night;

Wyfurge's letter blames the Clock; and more,
— Mrs Hammer reads with narrowed eyes —
he cites their agents in the docks;
they exist, he claims,
they are not shadows,
nor mere shades of dreams;

for they have disrupted reconstruction
of Port Dog's lower reaches;
the tower does not reach
half the height it should,
and so the water
in the flooded conurbations of
Port Dog's intended limits
does not recede, and worse —
the tower has become a joke among the Scythians.

Mrs Hammer, lawyer to the Empire,
charged by Imperial appointment
with the making of things right
here ponders, grimfaced,
the notion that somehow,
related to this intractable mire
that besets her waking hours,
are the dreams of light and shade
that she knows would devour her,
if she ever were to sleep at night.

*

THE SECRET WEAPON

The Secret Weapon, in a black, unblinking eye,
stares the auger down,
stares down the changeless height.

The Secret Weapon lies suspended on her gurney.
Below that glowering cloud, all black and strung,
the Secret Weapon holds aloof,
interred inside her shroud —

The Secret Weapon trundles forth,
alone in folds of falling, slitherine cloth.
Illiterate ink blows in, across from the north,
inclement weather in great,
awful gobs of incoherent sloth,
and shadows black as sin
that make no sense at all
are cast everywhere.

In neoclassical repose
the Secret Weapon rests a while, and waits;
the winding gear turns, and while
the torque is yet too green to pass
from the handle, near the feet reclined,
to the axles, where a training wheel waits,
in time the Enemy will come...

In dark clouds of falling silk and ink
and lines that red and thin
define the scene
to the satisfaction of the counting machines

(in Arabic and Roman)
in letters large and proud and strong,
that even on close inspection have no seams
and next to no interior doubt
as to what they mean;

The Secret Weapon is not so secret now;
parked in plain remorseless view,
she lies upon the gurney.

In one black eye,
the Secret Weapon tests the lie
of the tyrant's changeless height,
below the folds of falling ink,
descending like the night —

and now, and more, for all of time,
in one unblinking, black, untroubled eye,
the Secret Weapon turns her gaze
for all of time

to the endless secret
of the sky.

*

BY THE SAME AUTHOR

The Day of the Nefilim

PRE / POST / WHENEVER / ABOVE GROUND / UNDERGROUND
APOCALYPTIC SF

Paperback, Kindle, Epub

"There is nothing more joyous to me than discovering new, raw creativity. David Major, regardless of his hallucinogen/s of choice, is a rare find and a fun read. With a smidgeon of Douglas Adams he spends all of six pages before rearranging our world with a sledgehammer and sending us down into underground caves and underworld civilizations in a ship that sails the winds of time. While Major hints occasionally at the science and history behind his bizarre story, it almost doesn't matter as *The Day of the Nefilim* is a great book, a delightful fantasy and well worth the read..."

"Can't wait to read your next book... You would make Robert Anton Wilson proud, and Douglas Adams smile."

"It's an odd book..."

ADISTANTMIRROR.COM.AU